THE WEEPING SKY

THE WEEPING SKY

Lee Harding

CASSELL AUSTRALIA

CASSELL AUSTRALIA LIMITED
31 Bridge Road, Stanmore, New South Wales
30 Curzon Street, North Melbourne, Victoria

Copyright © 1977 Lee Harding

First published 1977
Jacket design and illustrations Michael Payne
Set in 11/13 Times Roman
Printed and bound by Times Printers Sdn Bhd, Singapore
F.1077

National Library of Australia
Cataloguing in Publication Data
Harding, Lee John, 1937-
  The weeping sky.
  ISBN 0 7269 3714 2
  I. Title.
A823.3

Contents

FOR IRENE,
WHO WAS THERE

ONE

The weeping sky

And so they came at last to an enchanted valley.

They had been advised to time their arrival for late afternoon, when the sun was low behind the transparent face of The Wall, and the valley stained with the terminal colours of the day.

Awed by this sudden brilliance, the two horsemen reined their mounts to a standstill. They became motionless silhouettes limned with an unnatural light, oblivious of the crowd of gawping onlookers surging around them. They sat thus for some time before the older man was moved to address the youth who rode with him.

"Well, Conrad," he said softly, "Would you not say this thing before us is a . . . miracle?"

The boy could not answer immediately. His whole attention had been caught and held by the apparition stretched midway across the valley. His keen eyes marked how it captured the long rays of the setting sun, amplified them in some curious manner, and mixed them with the tattered remnants of cloud scudding low across the horizon. This dazzling display of colour gave The Wall the appearance of an enormous stained-glass window suspended in the sky. Never before had the young student seen anything so strange, so beautiful. His mouth went dry; a flush crept into his cheeks; his body began to glow with excitement.

His companion waited patiently for him to reply. The grey-bearded features of the older man were wise and kindly, and denoted the cool, detached manner of a scholar. His

1

wide-brimmed felt hat and flowing burgundy-coloured cloak identified him as a person of some importance.

After a while he spoke again. "I said, Conrad, would you not say that this vision before us is indeed a 'miracle'?"

The youth made a wry face. He was only sixteen. This was his first Investigation undertaken outside the high walls of the College. But he firmly believed all that he had learned from Master Asquith and his colleagues.

He took a deep breath, and chose his words with care. "There can be no ghosts, no gods nor devils nor witches nor . . . 'miracles', such as we have been led to believe. Only a lack of proper information."

The older man nodded approvingly. "Well spoken, Conrad." He could see that the boy's pale, sensitive features were flushed with the glow that flooded the valley before them. His blond hair stood out from his face like a fiery halo. Despite his youth his eyes portrayed a passionate interest in their quest and, for the moment, in this supernal light, he struck a rather heroic image.

Master Asquith permitted himself a gentle smile. Young Conrad was his prize pupil. He felt sure he had chosen well when he asked the boy to accompany him. There were times when Conrad seemed wise beyond his years, a singular quality which set him apart from his fellows.

The Wall was a mystery they had come here to unrave And they had best be on about their business. Asquith urged his horse through the crowd of onlookers. "Come along, lad. Let us take a closer look at this . . . miraculous Wall."

About a hundred people had gathered along the eastern rim of the valley that afternoon. Most had arrived on foot from nearby Northbridge, the village that lay four miles distant. Some, however, came on horseback, having covered a much greater distance in order to bear witness to the 'miracle'. Others arrived in rickety old carts pulled by weary and aged oxen.

News of The Wall had spread swiftly through a land

hungry for a miraculous portent. It would only be a matter of time, Asquith reflected, before the valley was over-crowded with pious, footsore pilgrims, as well as every kind of degenerate. Unlike the innocent believers, the latter would be drawn here by the lure of easy pickings. And—he found—the presence of so many people would only hinder their Investigation. Therefore they had best proceed swiftly and quietly and complete their task before the rabble took over.

Earlier in the day, The Wall—for this was the name by which it was now known—was less spectacular. In the morning a man would have difficulty finding it, so discreetly did the dawn light reveal its mysterious substance upon the still air. But later in the day, when the languid autumn sun had wandered a short distance across the sky and hung low above the distant hills, The Wall threw back the sunlight so intensely that onlookers were forced, after a while, to turn away, lest they be robbed of their sight. And as the afternoon sun sloped towards dusk, the display of colour became awesome as the sun moved behind The Wall.

At first only a bright streak of vermilion marked the upper edge of The Wall. But as the sun sank lower, the valley was transformed into a blazing orange cauldron awash with the shifting patterns cast by The Wall. Individual details of the landscape became blurred and lost, swallowed up by the blaze of colour. The valley grew other-worldly, remote from everyday experience.

It was less than a mile across at its widest point, and per-haps four miles long. The mysterious Wall was stretched across the centre, north to south, its diffuse edges barely reaching the slopes on either side.

There was no road leading down into the valley, only a crude path worn into the ground by the solitary shepherd who worked these stunted pastures. And, as the two travellers descended into the fierce orange glow, it seemed to Conrad that their figures merged into an almost dreamlike anonymity. Horses and riders became part of the transfigured landscape so that it seemed—for a time, until their senses had adjusted—that they were moving not so much through a physical environment, but rather passing through an unfamiliar landscape of the mind. The effect was. . . disquieting.

Ahead of them were other travellers, some on foot, several on horseback. All moving slowly and purposefully, like themselves, to get a closer look at the 'miracle'.

The boy noticed that already a small township had begun to take shape on the floor of the valley. A few campfires stood out bravely against the overwhelming brilliance of the amplified sunset. Tents had been pitched here and there and some crude shelters assembled out of pieces of wood and cloth. Obviously some of the more devout pilgrims were determined to maintain a steady vigil. But their encampment made a tawdry sight.

Narrowing his eyes, Conrad could see some figures moving around, closer to The Wall. A few had formed islands of shadow while others wandered aimless and alone, describing awkward diagrams on the valley floor.

"Monks," Asquith explained. "From the monastery we passed."

They had left that place a good half-mile behind them on the road from Northbridge. Conrad recalled how it had reminded him of some stricken animal crouched low against the earth, as though it were trying to draw sustenance from the arid soil. As they had passed by the crumbling walls of what had once been a proud and famous monastery, he could not help but feel that the long hand of the drought had penetrated its walls to drain off whatever life was left inside. But the monastery belonged to another world, where objects and people retained their individuality and were not swallowed up by this fiery orange cauldron. . . .

As they rode on Asquith explained how it was common knowledge that the monks of St Germaine were convinced of

4

the divine nature of The Wall. They had already spread word to this effect and it was they, more than anyone else, who were responsible for the present array of sightseers. "And we can expect many more in the days to come," he grumbled, in a tone of voice unusual for him. He, too, found the light curiously unsettling.

An idle thought brought an amused expression to the boy's face. "Master Asquith," he said, leaning forward in his saddle, "if their theology indeed be true, then it might also be possible that they are deluded, and have spread the gospel of this 'miracle' on behalf of the Evil One instead of their One True God. Do you not find that amusing?"

Asquith nodded. "Aye." But he did not smile. His mind was on other things. Later, perhaps, he would properly appreciate the boy's perception.

The ground levelled out. They had reached the floor of the valley and let their mounts proceed at a cautious gait over the rough, uneven ground. They passed by several tents and shelters, cobbled together by groups of earnest pilgrims busily praying or jabbering among themselves. Above them, The Wall loomed immense and magnificent, holding them spellbound with its supernatural splendour. Farther on they drew abreast of the restless monks; only a few knelt in rapt adoration and practised prayer. The reason for this was soon apparent: the ground had become quite moist, unsuitable for enthusiastic genuflection. Asquith smiled. No wonder the worthy brothers of St Germaine had advanced no farther!

Now there was no one ahead of them. Asquith called a brief halt. With hands raised to protect their eyes from the fierce glare, they saw how a shallow lake had formed underneath The Wall. It glowed in the eerie light like a bowl of molten metal.

"Conrad, you have long leather buskins. I am not so well outfitted to investigate this lake. Well, lad—are you prepared to try?"

For answer the student quickly handed the reins of his

mare into his Master's safekeeping; then he dismounted eagerly. "I will do so at once, sir," he exclaimed, scarcely able to control his excitement. The sight of The Wall had filled him with wonder. Until now all his study, all his training, had been conducted inside the College. His world had been one of endless peering into microscopes, dissecting two-headed calves and other jokes of nature. Now, with one bold step, he was about to cross the frontier of theory and move into the practical realm of Scientific Investigation.

He set off.

He moved confidently, taking care to keep his eyes averted from the fiery face of The Wall. It was not that the phenomenon had instilled fear in him. His reactions were made up of equal parts of awe and curiosity. His training had been thorough. This mystery, dubbed 'The Wall', was much too grand to be taken in at a glance and weighed against a penny-worth of superstition. He was determined to make as close a study of its nature as possible. So he began to wade through the brackish waters of the lake.

Carefully shielding his eyes, he could see for the first time how The Wall glowed more strongly, like a solid sheet of glass, directly over the lake. But as it reached out on either side, the intensity of the light diminished, and eventually faded away into a shimmering mist at the extreme edges of the phenomenon. He judged this central portion to cover a good third of the valley, and the height of The Wall to be almost as great, making it roughly one quarter of a mile high. But even this was difficult to ascertain, for the upper limits of the phenomenon became as tenuous as its outstretched arms.

Before him, the bottom of The Wall merged with the shallow lake. He waded cautiously towards it, wondering how close he might get. From time to time he thought he could detect a fine network of lines criss-crossing its face. But they kept fading and then reappearing, so that he could not be sure if they really existed or were a visual illusion. He made a mental note to mention this to Asquith.

As he drew closer to The Wall he became aware of waves of warmth reaching out to him. And the light now pouring from the central portion of the phenomenon remained many times more brilliant than the dying sun it plundered.

It is acting like a lens, he thought. And then, amazed by the audacity of his deduction, thought again: *a lens!* The thrill of his discovery sent a shiver of excitement racing through him. College studies had made him familiar with the new and marvellous magnifying optics recently come out of Spain: the half-dozen or so the College possessed were among its most valued tools. And be perceived that this Wall, this mysterious vision, seemed to share similar qualities!

By now he was more than ankle-deep in muddy water. Still he advanced. The lake did not appear to be more than a few inches deep, but he moved warily, lest he stumble on the uneven and unseen ground.

He was perhaps a hundred yards from the shore. The waves of heat grew more intense with every step. He paused for a moment to make a detailed study of The Wall through half-closed eyes. The glare was noticeably less brilliant now and this enabled him to make a better observation. The network of fine lines had disappeared altogether—perhaps after all they had only been an illusion. He stood quite still for what seemed a long time, like one entranced, before he grew aware of an angry buzz of sound behind him.

Slowly he turned around.

It took him a few moments before his eyes adjusted to the different quality of the light. He saw that a group of monks now stood by the shore of the lake. A short distance to their left, Master Asquith waited anxiously for his return: he had not expected his pupil to make such an audacious foray into the lake.

The hooded figures of the monks gestured angrily at Conrad. He could hear, but could not make out the words of their angry muttering. He thought they looked like a group of irritable old women, waving their arms around.

"Come back . . . come back . . . come back . . . come back"—this seemed to be their garbled message. *"You have no right to be where you are. This is holy ground. You have profaned . . . come back. . ."*

If this was indeed their attitude, then Conrad chose to ignore it. He smiled—a trifle insolently— and resumed his progress. He was a small island of human consciousness moving through a lake the colour of molten copper under the baleful eye of The Wall.

After a while the angry muttering behind him grew still. The monks fell to brooding and marked his progress with awe and in silence. Glancing back, Conrad saw one of them make the Sign. He felt a mingling of contempt and tolerance for the monks. Unlike him, they had been taught to revere, never to question the true nature of the world they lived in. Therein lay their differences and the reasons for a mutual antagonism.

By now the water came up to his knees; it seemed unwise to advance farther. Besides, the waves of heat beating out from The Wall made it suddenly difficult for him to breathe the uncommonly humid air. Conrad felt strangely light-headed. It became increasingly difficult for him to focus his thoughts. He was reminded of another, earlier time: a warm summer day when the air had been filled with girlish laughter and he had tasted wine for the first time. . .

Enough. I have done enough for today. But almost as an afterthought he stooped and dipped the fingers of his right hand into the lake. He lifted them carefully and tasted the moisture on his fingertips with the tip of his tongue. He made a wry face. The water was salty. Not as salty as the sea, but certainly the tang lay on his tongue. Yet the nearest ocean was several hundred miles south of the valley. Could there be some deep subterranean connection between this lake and the distant sea? If so, how had it come into being?

8

These were matters he would discuss with Master Asquith.

While he pondered, the sun dipped slowly out of sight behind the western rim of the valley. The intolerable brilliance of The Wall began to fade; only its upper reaches retained traces of the former fire. Now it no longer looked like a wondrous stained-glass window; it was more like a fine mist flowing down into the lake.

Conrad shook his head in puzzlement. He turned around and made his way back to the shore. As his eyes once again adjusted, he saw the landscape begin to regain its former individuality. It was possible to make out stunted trees scattered here and there, and the small encampments stood out starkly in the valley. He could even read the dour expressions of the monks waiting by the edge of the lake.

He found this return to an everyday scene a little unsettling, so much had his thoughts been uncoupled from reality since his arrival in the valley.

The monks witnessed his return with a hostile silence. . . and a grudging admiration. Not one of them would have dared what he had done, and well Conrad knew it. He struck up a jaunty step when he was on dry ground again, and went to rejoin his Master.

Asquith was relieved to have him back. But he made no comment, simply handed back the reins of his horse.

As Conrad swung up into his saddle he felt a moment of surprise when he found his left leg was shaking. For no reason he could understand. He said briskly: "Our informants were correct, sir: the sky does truly weep. The waters certainly taste of salt."

Asquith nodded. He was deep in thought. He turned his horse away from the lake and motioned the boy to follow. "Now we had best seek out the shepherd we were told of. That is his dwelling—see, that house over there. The light is fading fast; we had best hurry. They say, Conrad, that he can tell us more about this Wall than any other man because he has watched it from the very beginning, when it was but a

9

fraction of its present size."

They rode off into the dusk. The monks watched them with anger in their hearts and a question in their simple minds. In each one of them there burned a flame of bitterness for these trespassers—and for all those who, they knew, would follow and dispute their claim that The Wall was a divine phenomenon.

But no doubt their Abbot would find ways with dealing with all those who scoffed.

TWO

The coming of The Wall

The shepherd's house lay about 400 metres from the lake, near the southern slopes of the valley. As the two horsemen closed the distance they could just make out in the fading light that it was a simple dwelling with a thatched roof and earthern walls. The wan light of a flickering oil lamp shone out through an open doorway. Nearby was a wooden barn, half-falling over from age.

Conrad glanced back over his shoulder and was not surprised to see that the crowd of onlookers was breaking up near the entrance to the valley. Now that the day's display was over, many of them would be making their way back to their homes.

Yet he could see that many had chosen to remain, and were even now making their way down into the valley to join others already encamped there.

As they drew close to the house he could see the shadowy form of a tall figure standing just outside the open doorway. A man who seemed to watch their approach with interest. His very stillness made Conrad uneasy. This looked like no shepherd he had ever seen.

Asquith reined his mount to a halt some distance from the house and quietly bade Conrad do likewise. It was from this close range that the light spilling out from inside the house lent the waiting figure a terrifying visage.

The man was a giant. He stood nearly seven feet tall and his features were so strong and fierce that they would not have disgraced a gargoyle. His eyes were dark and impenetrable. His hooked nose curved down until it almost touched his wide, cruel mouth. His lips were pulled back into what might have been a gesture of defiance. He was dressed in poor, travel-stained garments covered by a heavy coat that came down to his ankles, and a frayed turban was wrapped loosely around his great head. Underneath his coat, the cloth pulled back so that all might see it, he wore a wide, studded belt that carried an enormous curved sword, broader than a man's arm. They could not fail to notice that the giant's hand rested almost casually upon the jewelled hilt of this magnificent weapon, his fingers spread a little apart as though ready to grasp the deadly instrument at a moment's notice.

Asquith leaned towards Conrad, and whispered: "This is like no shepherd I have ever seen," he whispered. "The man's surely a Saracen—and very far from his homeland."

His words took Conrad by surprise. A Saracen! Many were the legendary tales he had heard of their great allies in the Crusades, but he had never seen one. He did not doubt for a moment his Master's surmise; Asquith always knew whereof he spoke. But the fact that they should confront this man so far from his homeland, in this strangest of all places, seemed strange indeed.

Asquith urged his mount a few paces forward. "Good evening," he called out politely. "I see by your mein that you are a Saracen. Welcome to our isle. I deem it an honour to meet one of our illustrious allies. We seek a shepherd here by the name of Angus Mallory. Have you seen such a man?"

He was met with silence. The giant did not move, nor did he betray by the slightest movement of his dark eyes that what had been said meant anything to him.

Another figure appeared in the doorway. "I am Angus Mallory," declared a tired voice. "What brings you here? As if I didn't know already! 'Tis The Wall, is it not? An' you come here loaded with questions. . . questions. . . *questions*."

12

"And coin," Asquith said softly, interrupting the old man's tirade with the simple jingling of a purse. The welcome sound put to a sudden stop to the shepherd's complaining.

Asquith let his horse step closer until the light from inside the house showed him clearly to the old man—and the Saracen. Conrad followed timidly behind.

"It is true that I would ask questions of you," Asquith went on, "but unlike some others, I am prepared to pay for such information as you may be prepared to give." He kept one eye on the giant, who still stood there without uttering a word.

The old shepherd took a few steps closer, and peered up at them in the half-light. "Who be ye?"

"I am Roger Asquith. This young man who rides with me is Conrad le Jeune. We are of the Guild of Scientists. We have come far from our College at Abingdon to make careful study of this thing you call 'The Wall'. Now, if we have your permission to dismount and enjoy your hospitality for a short while to discuss this singular event in some detail, you will be amply rewarded for your patience." He jiggled the purse again to add weight to his inducement.

"A Scientist, eh?" The old man shrugged his stooped shoulders. "Heard tell o' them. Not much, mind you. 'Cept that Mother Church don't take too kindly to thee." He sighed. "Well, come inside, come inside." He motioned them to dismount.

They did so, and tied the reins of their mounts to a stunted tree that grew close by the house. Then they followed Mallory inside. The Saracen watched them, but did not budge from his position outside the open door.

As Conrad had expected, the house consisted of only one large room. But much to his surprise he saw that the floor had been carefully inlaid with many smoothly polished stones, lending an air of comparative luxury to the simple dwelling. A fire burned fitfully in one corner. An old black

13

dog lay curled on the hearth; it raised a shaggy, indifferent head when they came in, regarded them for a moment, then went back to sleep.

There was hardly any furniture. A wooden table stood in the centre of the room, where the oil lantern gave off its welcome glow. There was only one chair and a footstool. A jumble of dilapidated cupboards was pressed against the opposite wall. As Conrad studied them he saw a mouse dart inside one of the open doors. He looked quickly away.

At the far end of the room, on his right, there was some kind of simple bed. In the flickering lamplight he could make out the figure of a man stretched out upon it, apparently asleep. A young boy sat beside him, looking up at the newcomers. It was impossible to distinguish their features in the wavering light, but both Master and student quickly associated them with the silent sentinel outside.

"I haven't much in the way o' furniture," the old man apologized. "A man like me, who lives alone. . . but you'll understand." A sudden shiver racked the shepherd's frail body. He hugged himself and muttered something about the nights being cold for this time of year, when in fact it was the most mild of evenings. "Time ter close the door," he mumbled.

He went outside and had a few quick words with the Saracen. The giant followed him in and took up a position just inside the house. Mallory closed and fastened the stout wooden door, then moved across to secure the heavy shutters across the solitary window looking out over the valley.

The Saracen stood with his legs braced slightly apart. He had not taken his eyes off the newcomers since he had stepped inside. If ever there was a bodyguard, Asquith mused, then this must certainly be the best he had ever met.

"Now, what is it that you want ter know?"

Both Master and student looked closely at the old shepherd for the first time. Angus Mallory was indeed old: three-score years and more had brought his stubborn spirit to heel and sewn deep furrows in his face. The long years of drought had hardened his spirit; a multitude of misfortunes had thinned his hair and grizzled his long, unkempt beard. He moved slowly, on one game leg—the legacy of an old wound and a reminder, every now and again, of a nobler past.

Mallory was a freeman. The valley was a fief he had won many years earlier from the Lord for whom he had fought. As young men, they had stood side by side against the Spanish invaders and many a time only swift action on his part had saved the young nobleman from death. And he had not forgotten Angus Mallory. Ah, but that had been in the golden springtime of their lives, before the truce and the partition of this fair isle. *One third,* he would often grumble to himself. *One third of our isle did we surrender to those devils!* But all that was long ago. For more than a quarter of a century now the two nations had lived happily together and prospered. They had even joined forces against the pagan Slavs when a false prophet rose up in the icy north of the world and declared a holy war against all Christians. For many years those barbarians had fought to claim the See of Adrian in the holy city of Athens, and only the strength of mighty allies had helped keep them back.

Asquith removed his wide-brimmed hat and placed it on the table. There was nothing to be gained by wasting time. He opened his purse and withdrew two small, silver coins. He handed them to Mallory. "We do not wish to take up too much of your time, but there are some things we desire to know. Unlike the worthy brothers at the monastery, we are not yet convinced of the divine nature of this Wall."

Mallory nodded and pulled a face. "Aye, them's a queer lot all right. And as for their Abbot. . ."

Asquith held up a hand. "I know only too well the nature of the Abbot of St Germaine, friend Mallory. Now, if you could perhaps begin by describing how The Wall looked when first you saw it. . .? Pietro the innkeeper at Northbridge where we stayed overnight, assured me that you were the only person who could describe the growth of this thing from the very beginning.''

The old man nodded. ''Aye, he be right there, sure enough. But he waters his ale, that Pietro. You have ter watch him.''

''Quite so.'' Asquith took up a position leaning against the wide mantelpiece above the smouldering fire. Conrad sat down at the table, his attention wandering self-consciously from the Saracen to the dim-lit couple at the far end of the room.

''Perhaps if you could begin?'' Asquith prompted.

''Eh?'' Mallory looked up. ''Oh, of course.'' He sat down on the stool facing Conrad, his hands clasped together on the table, staring deep into some private vision. ''You see, it really weren't nuthin' at first: just a bit o' dew danglin' in the air. . .''

He had stumbled upon it early one morning, only three weeks ago. He had been on his way back from the trickle of a creek that cut diagonally across the valley—it was his only source of water now. He had been favouring his game leg, cursing the old wound and in general railing against the long drought. Weighed down by the casks of water yoked across his shoulders, for a moment he thought he had blundered through a spider's web stretched between two stunted trees, all dappled with morning dew.

His simple mind was easily beguiled. He stopped for a moment and looked back the way he had come, expecting to find a large web spread before him, a part of it all tattered from his passage. But all he saw was a tiny cluster of water droplets suspended in the air. They were almost at eye-level and they sparkled prettily, just as he imagined diamonds would—for he had never seen such jewels.

He stepped backward in surprise and almost toppled over, precious casks and all. But he managed to maintain his precarious footing. The he carefully lowered the yoke and casks to the ground and moved closer to the strange dew.

16

The beauty of the tiny droplets entranced him. He wondered how they came to be there, and what supported them. Then he saw how they gradually ran together and formed tiny rivulets that made their way down to the ground. The soil directly underfoot was surprisingly moist, quite different to the rest of his arid valley. He stared at it in astonishment.

When he had summoned up sufficient courage, he reached out one shaking hand and gently gathered some of the droplets on to his fingers. He tasted them and found them sweet on the tongue. He closed his eyes; a tremor passed through him. His head became filled with an enormous wonder. He felt himself witness to one of God's miracles; he, Angus Mallory, had not been forgotten in the rough passage of the years. Overcome, he fell to his knees and began to pray.

The lonely and embittered man in him might have forsaken his God long ago, but the forgotten child never had. He asked for further signs of God's presence in the valley, but, although he remained there unmoving for what seemed like several long hours, no more were forthcoming. And yet the miraculous dew persisted.

Eventually his weary old bones protested at his posture. He staggered to his feet and began massaging life back into his aching limbs. He wondered what he should do next. And while he wondered the sun rose higher and he saw how the fine mist was spread out across the valley, the tiny droplets sparkling in the autumn sunlight. He could scarcely believe his good fortune. His thirsty pastures would have water at last. Was this God's way of announcing that the long drought had come to an end?

His mind, unaccustomed to serious thought, struggled to devise some course of action. For the first few days he hugged his miracle to him and carried news of it to no one. It was his secret. His alone. For it had been visited upon his valley, and none other.

But as the days passed and he marked how the wide

17

curtain of moisture grew and condensed and spread out even farther across the valley, and knew how the sunset became a time of aching, intolerable beauty, he came to believe that God had not intended him to keep this vision to himself.

He knew there were men outside his valley, men more learned than himself, who might make something of this Sign. So one morning he prepared himself and set off as fast as his game leg would allow, leaning heavily on a stout wooden staff and followed faithfully by his old hound, Rafe.

First he called at the monastery of St Germaine. He brought news of the miracle to the worthy brothers and bid them hasten to bear witness to its presence in his valley. But The Wall had not yet grown so high that the monks could see it peeping over the rim of the valley, so they laughed and joshed him good-naturedly. They tossed aside his garbled words as they would have done the ravings of any witless man. It was well known that the old shepherd had lived a solitary life for nigh on twenty years, ever since his wife died. This isolation must have addled his wits. Besides, these were hard times and their charity and patience were too often strained. They had no time to listen to the stammered dreams of an old man well-hewn for the grave. They told him to be-gone.

Mallory, outraged by their lack of interest, turned angrily away and set off in the direction of Northbridge. It was only four miles distant, but that was quite a journey for his old limbs. But the light of his vision burned fiercely within him and gave him new-found strength.

Northbridge was a small settlement set well apart from the mainstream of commerce. Like many similar towns and villages, it had been left stranded by progress and had been slowly dying for many years. Even so, surely they would listen to him there?

But his visit to Northbridge proved even more disastrous than his arrival at the monastery; at least the monks had retained a pretence of civility. The people of Northbridge were a ragged and suspicious lot. Over the past two years they had lost more than two-thirds of their population. Some had moved away to find work in one of the more prosperous northern towns. Others had been taken by the plague, which only last winter had uncurled itself from a long sleep and lashed out, scourging the countryside.

The few who remained in Northbridge were stragglers, weighed down with bitterness and consumed with inertia. Their lives had congealed into a dull routine. In much the same way that corrugations on a dirt road become hardened by the merciless sun, so had their hearts grown hard and unloving. They distrusted strangers and envied the wealthy merchants who passed through their village. They were aware, from time to idle time, that they and their dwellings were doomed, but there seemed to be nothing they could do to prevent this. All the wise men had left long ago: only fools remained. Northbridge would soon join the dozens of deserted villages scattered throughout the land. It was into this inhospitable place that Angus Mallory limped with his great news. . .

"A miracle!" he called out, pausing outside the local inn. "I tell all of you, I have seen a miracle in my valley!"

It was shortly before noon—not the best of times to disturb the villagers from their idleness. Most of the menfolk sat around drinking ale. These people, men and women alike, were the sorry dregs of time, a poor audience for the impassioned old shepherd. Yet he tried to move them.

"Listen," he beseeched them, gasping for breath and and leaning heavily on his staff. "I 'ave great news. Great news!"

And so he poured out his tale. His long trek had left him weak and exhausted, but his tongue was afire with an unaccustomed eloquence.

At first they greeted his story with scorn and derision. They knew the shepherd as a man of simple means and mind: a recluse, given to day-dreaming, whose words were best taken lightly, it at all. They had often made sport of the old fool whenever the mood took them.

When they grew weary of his ranting a group of louts decided to make fun of him. They howled him down, then gave him a rough tumbling in the dry dust of the main street. They kicked away his staff and tossed his frail body back and forth between them, laughing all the time. One or two heavy blows were struck. And when they were tired of their game they left him lying in the dust like a discarded sack and resumed their drinking.

Rafe had crept quickly away when the bullying began. Like his master, he was old and infirm, and he cringed from the pain he knew these people could inflict. When the dust and the shouting had settled, the dog crouched safe beneath an old cart, observing Mallory's disgrace from a distance.

The old man lay quietly, nursing his bruises and cursing his tormentors under his breath. A small mongrel wandered over, sniffed around him for a moment, raised a hind leg and pissed, then moved off. This drew a rush of laughter from the people gathered outside Pietro's inn.

Mallory groped around until he found his staff. He managed to lever himself upright, and stood there shaking after his ordeal. He ached all over and his left eye was already badly swollen. But his heart still burned with the strength of his vision. He wondered why he had taken the trouble to come to Northbridge. Where, among this dreary lot of souls, would he find anyone willing to listen to him?

The village festered quietly in the noonday sun. Mallory moved off down the street, in no particular direction, still hopeful of finding an honest ear. A group of grubby children followed him. They were a tough lot, every bit as unpleasant as their parents. Innocence seemed never to have touched them. Their flesh was undernourished; it stared out here and there through their tattered clothing.

They caught him unawares with their sudden flurry of sticks and stones. They abused him soundly in a manner copied from the louts, until finally the shepherd rounded upon them in a fury, waving his wooden staff and raving at them to begone. They laughed at him and urged their dogs after him. Rafe whimpered and got quickly out of the way; he was much too old to fight his own kind. Mallory cursed and tried to drive the pack away with his staff.

"Begone!" he cried. "Begone, you wretched curs!" He caught several of them a stinging blow across the skull. They howled and retreated. The remainder stood their ground and snarled, but came no closer.

Even the children backed away from his wrath; they had never before seen such a fierce light in an old man's eyes. They had thought the shepherd weak and finished; they had no way of knowing that he was driven by a divine vision.

"Go back to your sheep, old man!" Pietro called out from the doorway of his inn. "And have yourself a goodly portion of ale or wine before you go. It will help soothe your aches and ease your addled wits." He laughed then, along with his customers; but there was at least a touch of compassion in him that set him apart from the rest of the villagers. "Go home now," he said more gently, "while the sun still shines."

At this point in his story, the old man paused. Asquith and Conrad waited silently. The shepherd's narrative had given them a vivid picture of the dusty village street and the old man persecuted by the unfeeling villagers and their dogs.

At last Mallory resumed his tale. A miracle The Wall might be, but the Lord gave no sign that he even knew or cared that word of it was spread abroad. Mallory quietly damned the people of Northbridge and left them to their sorry fate. He set off home, and Rafe crept after him, tail between his legs.

Time will show them, he thought. A smile crept over his battered features. Let them make fun of him and abuse him; let their children set their mangy curs after him. *Time will tell them what I could not.* Soon the miracle would be plain

21

enough for all to see. He was content to wait.

And in time this came to pass. Travellers arriving from the north brought with them news of an unearthly glow in the afternoon sky only a few miles from the village. And the monks at the monastery of St Germaine were quick to announce that it was a Sign from the Lord.

The people of Northbridge remembered what the old shepherd had tried to tell them. Only a few recalled how badly he had been mistreated. And for want of something better to do they wandered off to the valley, to see for themselves if there was indeed some substance to these wild tales.

But the monks were there first. In a matter of days The Wall had grown to such a size that its upper edge was visible above the rim of the valley. And while some of them marvelled at the nature of the miracle, a few felt afraid when they saw how the sunsets were transformed into scenes of unearthly beauty; uneasy when the glory beckoned them from their cloisters. . .

They came and they worshipped, for this was in their nature, and it was only a matter of time before they were joined by pilgrims from far-off places. News of the miracle spread with astonishing speed. The number of pilgrims and eager sightseers grew steadily, and sleepy Northbridge found itself jolted out of its inertia and enjoying the briskest trade in years.

Collectively the village took a deep breath, found time to give thanks and praise the Almighty, then got ready to squeeze all they could from the purses of the many visitors streaming through the streets. Someone even had enough presence of mind to reopen the old church at the bottom of the main street. For nine long years it had languished unused while dust and cobwebs settled over it. Now everyone found they could enjoy the luxury of bringing their sins up to date.

And all the time the land underneath The Wall grew fat and gorged itself upon the moisture trickling from the sky. Soon the shallow lake began to form directly underneath the phenomenon. At first it was as clear and as pure as the first tiny droplets Mallory had tasted, and the old shepherd had rejoiced in his good fortune.

But there came a day when the waters of this newly-formed lake acquired a brackish, sullied look, and he approached it uneasily, his casks yoked over his bony shoulders.

The old shepherd's eyes had narrowed bitterly when he recalled how his 'miracle' had betrayed him. "Soon all my land will be useless," he groaned, and turned to Asquith helplessly. "Tell me, Master Scientist, what sort of miracle is't that sows a man's land with salt water and makes of him a mockery—and a pauper?"

Asquith bowed his head. The old man's story had moved him deeply. He wished that he could find some ready answer to ease the old man's mind, but he knew that he could not. After a moment he looked up. His face was drawn and uncertain in the flickering lamplight. "I cannot provide you with an explanation. Not yet. But we are here, my young friend and I, to find one."

"An explanation? Aye, you may find one in your cleverness. And then again, you may not. But can my land be saved?"

Asquith shook his head. "That is something we will have to find out. First we must investigate this phenomenon you call The Wall and then—"

The Scientist was interrupted by the sound of a deep moan from the far end of the room. Conrad looked quickly around and saw that the sleeping man had rolled over and was muttering restlessly. In the wan light he could see that the man's face was hideously scarred—and his garments those of a knight of the realm.

The youth by his side leant forward and spoke some soothing words into the man's ear, gently stroking his brow at the same time. The man continued to shift about restlessly for a few moments, then gradually subsided. Once he reached up

23

and gripped with one gnarled hand the soft white hand that stroked his brow. He mumbled something, then seemed to fall asleep again.

"These are pilgrims I've given board for the night," Mallory hastened to explain. "They have come far—very far. Ah, it is a sad thing. Sad indeed . . ." He shook his head in a weary gesture.

Asquith smiled wrily. It was obvious now that his was not the first coin to pass into the wily old shepherd's hands. Mallory's account, moving though it was, held the ring of an oft-repeated tale.

Conrad got up from his seat by the table. The memory of the knight's deeply-scarred face had aroused in him a curiosity, and a desire to give help, if he could. He walked the length of the room, aware that the Saracen's eyes were following him. The laboured breathing of the man lying on the bed sounded loud in the quiet room.

He came to a stop beside the bed. The youth was still staring down at the unconscious man, continuing to massage his brow.

Conrad said gently, "Is something the matter with this man? He seems gravely injured. If we might be of some assistance?"

The youth looked up. And much to his surprise, Conrad discovered that, despite the dark, close-cropped hair and boy's clothing, he was staring into the face of a young girl scarcely older than himself.

For a moment she eyed him defiantly, as though he were an enemy. Then her face relaxed; and now he saw that her features had acquired the drawn, dispirited quality of one who has grown accustomed to the grim business of mere survival.

It was very still inside the house.

He said again, more gently before, "If there is anything we can do?"

She did not answer.

THREE

A time of portents

Conrad glanced again at the ruined face of the man on the bed, then back to the girl. Even in the flickering lamplight her face was pale, her dark eyes lustreless; his presence had barely aroused her interest. Her cheeks were sunken, the bones showing sharply through the skin. Her short hair was grubby and plastered to her scalp with the grime of many days of travel.

He studied her clothes. She wore an old jacket, frayed in many places, and under it a coarse shirt such as any farm boy might wear. Her long grey trousers were travel-stained, tucked into a pair of battered old boots. When Conrad contrasted all this with the crisp Guild clothes he wore, he felt curiously ashamed.

He took a courteous step back and removed his cap. "I am Conrad le Jeune," he said, speaking softly and making a small bow. "The man you see with me is Master Roger Asquith, whom I have the honour to serve. We are of the Guild of Scientists. Please do not doubt our sincere desire to be of help."

Now the girl stood up, head held high, chin slightly outthrust. Conrad was a few inches taller, yet they faced each other as equals. There was pride in her stance and a fire in her eyes that belied her appearance. She allowed her right hand to brush against her open jacket; he caught a glimpse of the dagger sheathed at her waist.

"I am Donella de Vargas," she said proudly. "This man lying here is my father, Ramon. He was once a lord and

25

knight of this realm, but his long absence from this isle, fighting God's war, cost him everything he held dear.''

The man moaned again in his troubled sleep. The girl sat down at once and resumed stroking his brow with the most tender of gestures. Then she spoke again, resuming her tale. ''When he arrived home wounded, like so many of his fellow Crusaders,'' she went on, without looking up,'' he found that his castle and lands were no longer his. They had been usurped by others. His wife—my mother—was murdered. Some say this foul deed was done while she was defending our home. As for his daughter. . .'' her shoulders moved in a pathetic little shrug—''he found her working as a serving wench in a common tavern, trying to keep herself alive.'' Immeasurable bitterness underscored these last words, and when she looked up, Conrad saw hatred burning in her dark eyes. She nodded towards the Saracen. ''Do not mind Hakim. He will not harm you, unless he is provoked. He has been my father's faithful squire for many long years. Without him I doubt if my father would ever have made his way home.''

The girl went on. ''These Slavs captured Hakim once—they held him long enough to cut out his tongue. That is why he stays so silent. Ah, those people from the north are no better than beasts, and they are driven in their conquests by the greatest beast of all!'' She almost spat these words; Conrad was astonished that so much fury could be bottled up inside such a frail young girl.

She looked down at the man on the bed and gently placed one hand against his scarred cheek. ''And my poor father.'' For the first time he detected a break in her voice as she went on: ''They near-blinded him with fire. Now he can see only vague shadows and different shades of brightness: nothing else. I have become his eyes. I often wonder if it was for this reason alone that I was spared, when I might have died with my mother when those fiends invaded our castle. . .'' Her voice trailed away. She bowed her head, remembering deeds

26

she could never speak of.

None of this came as any surprise to Conrad. He had heard many a similar tale, of knights losing their house and lands while abroad. The country was in the hands of a witless king, and titles and property changed hands with surprising ease for the right amount of coin. Yet for all this he was left with a great admiration for her courage.

"You are Spanish?" he said. She nodded, without looking up. "You speak English very well."

"I have had much practice," she said bitterly. "I was eight when my father left for the War, thirteen when he returned. That was just over two years ago. I have had much opportunity to learn since then. Out of necessity, you understand."

The student nodded dumbly. Every time he spoke it seemed to him that his words sounded lame and unsympathetic. Her plight was such that he lacked the ability to express his pity. Instead he said, "And you have come here then, like all the others, to see this vision in the valley?"

"It was my father's wish, He seeks. . . he *needs* to have some proof that God exists before he dies. He found none wherever he fought. And it is through my eyes that he will discover what there is to see. We arrived only yesterday: already I have described much to him of this 'miracle'."—There could be no mistaking her inflexion; The Wall did not seem to have impressed her as much as it might have.

"What do you make of it?" Conrad asked.

She shrugged. "I find it an impressive spectacle. More so than the Northern Lights. Have you seen them?"

He shook his head. "No. . . but I have heard of them.—Are they not high in the sky, instead of being close to the ground, as this Wall is?"

"Aye, that is true enough."

Donella's father moaned deeply again. It was a pitiful sound. His daughter looked down at his ravaged face and

27

said, with scarcely a trace of emotion, "He is dying, Conrad le Jeune. And I think it would not be right if he were to die without . . . without something. Do you understand? I might . . . I may have to lie to him a little." Her voice dropped to a whisper as she said this. "Then he will pass from this world feeling happier than he has since he first left this land."

He saw no trace of tears in her eyes, but her grief was so great it was almost tangible. Averting his eyes for a moment he noticed that clean straw had been neatly arranged on the floor beside the bed, and some heavy blankets placed nearby.

"How long do you plan to stay here?" he asked.

Donella looked at him squarely. "The old shepherd has kindly provided us with shelter for—oh, a few days. Until my father is. . . satisfied." He guessed from her expression that she would do her best to ensure that this would be soon, so that she could take her ailing father to. . . wherever he needed to be. The prospect depressed the young student, and made him realize how cosseted he had been for so many years inside the high walls of his College. There was much he had yet to see of the cruel and barbarous ways of the world.

"Why did you not stay at the monastery?" he asked. "Surely they would take better care of you—"

Something close to fury blazed momentarily in the girl's otherwise expressionless eyes. "*The monastery*? Do you think that people such as we could buy our way in there with our pitiful small coin? No, it is gold and silver they seek—the sort of coin your Master carries." Her voice dropped towards the end of her tirade, but this did not help him to feel any less ashamed of their wealth—for such it must appear in the eyes of this poor girl.

"I am sorry if we have distressed you," he apologized. "But I hope you will accept my assurance that we are prepared to be of any assistance to you and your father, should you ever have need of us. Please, do not be too proud to accept such an offer. These fine clothes you see"—he ran his fingers down the side of his jerkin and twirled his felt cap lightly around his fingers—"they are a small deception. In order to carry out our work undisturbed by wily Mother Church, we must disguise ourselves as wealthy and respectable merchants. Mark you well, Donella, our purses are not as bottomless as they may seem." This last he whispered to her in secret. "You are prepared to lie to ease your father's passage into the next world; so must we use deceit to mask our motives. The Church does not take kindly to our Guild."

Her face softened a little in the lamplight. "I. . . I have heard of your Guild," she said softly. "I have heard that it is your sworn duty to prove that there is no God, and that this is why the Church looks upon your work with such disfavour. Surely it is arrogance to assume that?"

"Nay, lady, that is not true: it is leagues away in every direction from our cause. We seek to understand the nature of God *and* the world, so that mankind need not be weighed down with superstition. Why, our greatest Master of all, Robert Grost, has writ that there can be no proper theology without a true understanding of nature, because it is through nature that God manifests Himself. Does that seem blasphemous, Donella? That alone is our purpose: we do not seek to overthrow the Church, but to open all men's minds to the marvels of nature—and bring them to a better understanding of God. And if, by the same token, we break the chains the Church has bound around men's minds, then I see no great harm can come of it. Believe me, Donella, what men now call the "supernatural' is only the natural world misunderstood. It is our task, the task of our Guild, to understand as much as we can, and what we cannot—well, that we record in the hope that future generations will succeed where we have failed. Knowledge grows; in time, many things which we fear and do not understand will become plain, and no longer seem frightening."

Donella heard him out politely, but seemed unwilling to make any comment. He eyed her warily. "What say you now about our Guild?"

She looked away. "I do not care for the Church." She did not explain why. "As for your Guild, I have listened to what you have told me. If it be true, then I wish you well. And I assure you I will bear your kind offer of assistance in mind." She turned away from him then, her eyes intent upon her sleeping father, indicating there was nothing further she wished to discuss. Conrad did not feel offended. On the contrary, he felt quite satisfied by her response.

"Make sure that all your provisions and valuables are inside," he advised, before taking his leave. "I do not trust the likes of some I have seen outside."

Without turning around she answered, "We have already done so. Our horses and our cart are locked in the barn. Hakim will keep watch. That one never sleeps, even when his eyes seem to be closed."

"Then you are well served. I bid you good night. . . Donella de Vargas."

"Good night, Conrad."

But still she did not turn to face him.

Asquith was still deep in conversation with the old shepherd. Conrad went over to where the Saracen stood like a sentinel before the closed door. "Take good care of your mistress, Hakim," the young man advised. "I fear for her safety while she remains in this valley—and for all of you. Her disguise may easily be detected. . ."

The giant nodded sagaciously. For the first time Conrad saw a slight relaxing of the Saracen's fearful visage; he felt that he had been accepted. He smiled, and joined his Master.

"I am deeply grateful for having heard your tale," Asquith was saying to the shepherd. "Indeed, it is most sad that the water contains so much salt, but perhaps in time this will become less."

From the grim expression on Mallory's face, it was obvious to Conrad that the old man doubted the situation would ever improve.

Conrad leaned close and said quietly, so that only Asquith

could hear. "That young one over there is a *girl*. Scarce fifteen years, I would guess, and caring for a near-blinded father."

"So I have gathered," Asquith replied, a trifle gruffly. "Not all your words were inaudible. Besides, Angus Mallory has already told me of their predicament; he is kind and generous to offer them sanctuary. I doubt if the monastery would have taken them in."

"The girl seemed sure of that."

"Aye. However, they seem sure of what they are about—and I would not like to fall out with their Saracen. Well, let us move along now, Conrad." Asquith stepped back from the fireplace and drew his cloak around him. "We may need to do some persuading before we are allowed shelter in the monastery, so we had best be on our way." He turned and gripped the shepherd firmly on the shoulder. "And thank you, Angus Mallory, for giving us your time. . . and for your story. Take care of yourself. You may have already experienced some difficulties with the monks and sightseers churning up your land, but mark you this: the first-comers are better than those who will follow. Now, we must be off. Good night!" He waved his wide-brimmed hat and bowed courteously to Donella at the far side of the room.

The Saracen stood aside and opened the heavy wooden door, and Asquith passed out into the night. Conrad paused in the open doorway, casting a quick backward glance into the room. He was rewarded by seeing the girl's gaze following him. He looked at Hakim. The giant nodded, as though to reassure him that all would be well. The boy followed his Master outside.

The air was autumn-mild. The sky was clear and stretched over the valley was something that looked vaguely like a mist. During the night hours, this was all that remained of The Wall. In a while, when the moon rose, it would take on a soft silver face and charm the pilgrims who had pitched

31

their tents or slept out in the open. Certainly it was a most curious phenomenon.

They remounted and rode slowly out of the valley, taking care to avoid any encampments. But the boy found that the sight of so many friendly fires scattered throughout the night, and the gentle sounds of song and prayer, brought a much needed respite to his troubled soul. He was a devoted student of this new thing called Science, yet there were still secret parts of himself he had not properly sorted out. It all revolved around the question of belief, or the lack thereof. . . in Science as well as Mother Church.

The monks had already departed, depriving the valley of their doleful faces and pious humility. It was obvious they resented the presence of anyone else in the valley, that they had come to regard The Wall in all its manifestations as a message from God to His Church on earth; even the fact that Mallory had first witnessed this miracle was a constant annoyance. They doubted not that their Abbot, (who thirsted after glory in a manner quite unbecoming to his vocation), would eventually do something about the old man.

Asquith and his pupil took the narrow path out of the valley until they found the road that led back to North-bridge. By then the moon had risen; this made it easier for them along the dusty highway. Eventually they caught up with the straggling line of monks on their homeward journey. They sensed hostility and, as usual, chose to ignore it and rode on past them. Ahead, they could just make out the dark shape of the monastery set against a backdrop of stars.

The monastery had been built on a small rise. For miles around, the land was as flat and featureless as a tabletop. Far to the north, beyond the horizon, it rose gradually into foothills that eventually merged into a wide, snow-capped mountain range.

The windows of St Germaine winked at them through the

night with a flickering amber glow. The colour reminded Conrad of torchlight, of incense. . . of other things he would have liked to forget.

We are moving into the enemy's camp, he thought. He felt uneasy, but then—what better place to conceal oneself? He had faith in Master Asquith to bluff his way through, as he had done many times before. The Church was easily fooled by the swirl of an expensive cloak and the clink of coin.

As they approached the monastery, bearing away from the road, they drew abreast of another long line of monks making their solemn way in the direction of the valley. Their faces were illuminated by the many torches they carried; their movements seemed more resigned than purposeful.

"Ho, there!" Asquith called out, reining his mount to a halt. "Why are you off to the valley at so late an hour, good fathers?"

Their leader paused for a moment and looked up. "We are the Abbot's night watch," he explained. "We go to pay homage to the miracle God has sent down to us."

The monks filed past and continued on their way. The moon had etched with silver the small portion of The Wall visible above the valley; it seemed to beckon them like a departed spirit.

They watched until the flickering torches met up with the other group of monks returning from their daytime vigil. Then Asquith dug his heels into his mount and rode on to- wards the monastery. Conrad followed.

•   •   •

They were well met at the main gate. The Master's fine clothes and commanding manner assured them of a good welcome. And the clink of silver was always a helpful latchkey.

"I am a merchant, Roger Asquith by name," he told the monk peering out through the portal. The lie was a ritual that came easily to any of the Guild who embarked upon an

Investigation. "This is my apprentice, Conrad le Jeune. We require lodgings for the night. Perhaps for more than one night, if this can be arranged. We have coin to pay with."

"I am Brother Anselmo," the monk replied. He had a puffy, kindly face, with large round eyes and red cheeks. "If you will wait a few moments, I will confer with the Abbot."

Whatever passed between Brother Anselmo and his superior could not have been of any great import; very soon the monk came hurrying back. The gate was swung open.

"My lord Abbot bids you welcome," Brother Anselmo exclaimed, "and says you may stay as long as you desire. Please come in."

The large wooden hostelry outside the walls of the monastery had long ago fallen into disrepair. These were hard times and travellers an uncommon sight; Master Asquith and Conrad looked forward to comfortable lodgings inside the walls.

Brother Anselmo showed them where to stable their horses, then led them to their quarters. They passed through the main dormitory and down to the far end where they were admitted into a large, pleasant room.

The air smelled of the freshly-brewed ale which was the monastery's chief industry. Asquith smiled, thanked the monk for his assistance, and slipped a coin into his palm along with another of much larger denomination which he knew would find its way into the Abbot's coffers.

There was only one bed.

"If you will wait but a moment," said Brother Anselmo, "I will see that you are attended to in the proper fashion." He scurried off in search of extra bedding.

A short time after two young novices appeared. The first carried a small wooden pallet which he laid on the floor beside the main bed. His companion brought a bundle of heavy blankets. This done, they both retired.

Conrad's face had gone white when he saw them. There was something so mechanical, so devoid of life in their move-

34

ments, and for a moment he was stricken by the thought that he had once looked like them.

The boys returned with armfuls of fresh, clean straw which they proceeded to arrange on the pallet, then covered it with a blanket. Two heavy quilts were left to one side, and several pillows. Finally, two large candles were lit. Then the novices departed, wishing them a good night's sleep.

There followed a long silence.

"Well, Conrad," Asquith said eventually, a touch of weariness attending his words, "here we are, safe inside Mother Church. And I must confess that I am sorely tired. More so in mind than body, but weary nonetheless." And without another word he took himself to bed, shrugging off his heavy cloak and jacket and letting his boots fall heavily to the stone floor.

They both slept clothed; it was a habit all Scientists quickly grew accustomed to. Flight might be necessary at a moment's notice, if a deception was found out. Yet for the moment they seemed safe enough.

Conrad lay down on his pallet and stared up at the shadows dancing on the high ceiling. The simplicity of his bed did not bother him. He had slept on many a worse mattress. *Aye, and with only a cold stone underneath me and no cushion for my head.* But these were better days now; he pushed such thoughts out of his head. Idly his mind wandered back to the night before when they had spent the evening at Pietro's tavern in Northbridge.

What a fiery, argumentative evening it had been! The entire village was in a turmoil. There had never been anything as spectacular as The Wall to stir the people's simple minds.

It was a time of portents. As a child, Conrad had been constantly under the impression that the world was coming to an end, so weird and wonderful were the tales he had heard. Such stories had continued right to the present day. It was part of the business of Science to check out and evaluate such tales, to discover what substance, if any, lay about them, and in what manner the facts had been misunderstood.

In Abershire, Pietro had told them, villagers had scattered in fright from a three-headed dog running crazy through the town. Reports varied, but there seemed to be consensus that from each great head protruded a large, slavering tongue and sharp, pointed fangs. Some said the multiple eyes were terrible to behold, and that they burned with fire.

In nearby Weyton, black rain was said to have fallen for three days and three nights and two babes had been born with horned heads—mercifully to die within minutes of their birthing. Great fissures had opened in the dried-up river bed of Celadon and fire and smoke had belched forth from deep within the earth for seven days and seven nights. Elsewhere, fish had fallen from the sky, along with showers of toads and dead sparrows. Rivers had run uphill and hot stones had rained down on hapless villagers.

So the stories went. They were like so many the student had heard throughout his life; only now it was his vocation to pay more attention to such tales than he would have in the past. The College at Abingdon had documented thousands of such incidents. Many had turned out to be tall tales invented by imaginative liars eager to beget a rumour. Others had been explained away as highly imaginative reports of quite simple, everyday phenomena. But there were some for which no explanation had been found. Still, the records had been kept, in the hope that future generations might find them of some use. That was the way the College worked.

In such hard times as these, history showed that the people looked to heaven for a Sign. Seers cried out that the earth was indeed dying, and that people were witnessing The Last of The Years. Soon the ground would writhe and shudder and deliver up its dead. A mighty voice would thunder from on high and they all would be judged according to their works.

Yes, it was a time of portents. But some were sceptical:

36

those who had survived the plague and its aftermath had seen the worst that life had to offer and were less easily gulled. Yet there could be no denying that this was time of sudden death and danger; a time when life was at its cheapest, filled with broken dreams and a callous indifference towards other men. A time when dreadful imaginings took root in credulous minds. A time without joy, without hope. A time of terrible hardship for all but a few.

A time of portents.

And I have seen such a vision, Conrad mused, *such as I would never have thought possible.*—What would they make of it on the morrow?

Asquith was already snoring softly, sound asleep. The boy covered himself with only one blanket and slowly drifted off. The last conscious image that floated in his mind was the pale face of the young girl in the shepherd's house. . .

●   ●   ●

In his study, high up in the tower that dominated his lodge, the aged, gaunt-faced Abbot of St Germaine paced nervously to and fro. His hands were clasped so tight behind him that the knuckles showed white. His eyes were wild and staring, his lips drawn into a hard line. Sometimes they moved with a jerky rhythm as he quickly muttered a stream of prayers. Specks of saliva sprayed from his chin, as he tossed his head with rapid, bird-like movements. He was in a very agitated frame of mind. Although his eyes were open wide, it was obvious they were focused upon some inner vision.

Sometimes he would cease his pacing for a moment and look out of his window, where the narrow strip of the silver Wall shimmered over the rim of the valley. He imagined it was watching him, fixing him with a baleful eye, as though bearing witness to all the unpleasant things he had been forced to do in the name of the Church. Then he muttered again under his breath and resumed his nervous pacing. *If this*

37

be the beginning of Judgement, he kept thinking. . . but, oh! that it were not!

Trapped by his own inner torment, it seemed to the Abbot that through the agency of The Wall, all the Hosts of Heaven were gathering to impeach him for the crimes he had committed against mankind in the name of Mother Church.

What could he do? Was it still too late for atonement?

The investigation begins

Donella woke with the dawn. It was still and quiet inside the shepherd's house. Her father slept peacefully beside her. His breathing was regular; the dark spectres that often intruded upon his dreams had given him some respite. Donella nearly always slept soundly now. She had wrestled long enough with her own particular nightmares; if they had not been completely subdued, then at least she had learned to accept them. Now it was only occasionally that they disturbed her sleep. She had learned much from the Saracen. How to endure . . .

In the far corner she could see Mallory lying on his bed of straw, a heavy blanket drawn around him. He was snoring softly, his old dog curled up against his back for warmth. The fire had long since gone out and the first flush of dawn was creeping in through the chinks in the shutters. She crept out of bed, fully clothed, and quickly pulled on her boots and made her way to the door. She carried a threadbare blanket over her left arm and a scrap of cotton in her hand. Carefully lifting the stout wooden bar that kept the door securely locked, she slowly opened the door and slipped outside into the brisk morning air.

The valley was still. The people who had stayed overnight were all fast asleep, the monks huddled together close by the shore of the lake.

Donella took in a deep breath of the cool morning air. Usually this was the time of day she liked most, the time when she felt free from care and gave no thought to what the coming hours would bring. But today was different. There was a feeling of tension abroad; she could not be sure if it was present in the valley or if it come from within herself.

Scarcely had she set foot outside than the figure of Hakim, crouched to one side of the doorway with a blanket draped around him, opened his eyes and made to stand up. The gentle pressure of her hand on his shoulder assured him this was not necessary. She pointed in the direction of the small creek that curved around behind the house, and made washing motions with her hands. Hakim nodded; he understood. He slid back on his haunches, but his eyes were open. Donella knew that he could sleep standing up, if necessary. No man alive would ever take him by surprise: he always kept a part of his mind alert for danger.

She made her way around the side of the house, unlocked the barn door and spent a few moments patting and whispering to their three horses. She always gave a little extra attention to her beloved Feronia—her father's gift when he had come back from the Wars. The beautiful dark-brown mare had never been meant to haul a two-wheeled cart, but her father's illness was such that he could not endure many hours in the saddle. So, during their long journey from the south, he had spent more than half their travelling time lying on the bed his daughter had prepared inside the cart, with his own horse trailing along behind, hitched to the back. Donella held the reins of her fair Feronia and the Saracen always rode a little ahead of them, scouting around for signs of danger.

Donella left the horses and hurried outside. Already the sky was growing brighter. She looked up to where The Wall had been, but the moon had long since set and the sun had not yet risen; she had to look very hard before she could locate it, and then it was so vague and insubstantial, it seemed nothing more than a fine morning mist.

The land sloped gently away from the house towards the narrow trickle of a creek. She did not wish to move too far away, and chose a place where the water was very shallow and only a few feet wide, but clear and fresh where it ran over a layer of shining pebbles. There was a rock nearby. She unsheathed her dagger and rested it on the stone. Then she quickly undressed, shivering in the chill morning air. She knew the water would be icy at first—and it was—but she had not bathed since they had set out on their pilgrimage, ten days ago.

She knelt down by the edge of the creek. Teeth chattering, she took the cloth and plunged it into the water, using it to bathe the grime and sweat from her body. The shock of the water took her breath away. But after a while her clean, fresh skin began to tingle so deliciously that she forgot the cold. Oh, it was so good to feel clean again!

She doused her short hair over and over again with the water, scrubbing at it with her fingertips until both they and her scalp were sore. The water cascading down from her head stung her small breasts and made her gasp.

The sky had grown gradually lighter while she bathed. When she was finished she squeezed out the cloth, used it to wipe off as much of the moisture as she could from her tingling body, and then she sat down on the nearby rock, with the blanket wrapped around her.

She sat quite still, waiting for the warmth of her body to evaporate the remaining moisture from her skin, and for the blanket to absorb most of it. Her breasts ached from the exposure, but gradually this not unpleasant pain diminished and she sat cocooned in a peaceful silence. Her teeth stopped chattering; she managed to smile. That was the best bath she had had in ages! *Here,* of all places. . . .

For a few delicious moments she closed her eyes and fell into a drowse, musing on the more pleasant aspects of the last few hours. When she opened her eyes again and looked up she realized with a shock that true dawn was upon her. Soon others would be awake and abroad in the valley. Had not Conrad warned her about the type of people to expect out there?

Already she could hear the first faint sounds of voices coming to her from a distance. She dressed quickly in her boy's clothing, picked up the dagger resting beside her and sheathed it carefully. Then, with the old blanket once more draped over her arm, she marched jauntily back to the house.

● ● ●

"Donella? Is that you?"

Her father was awake and sitting up anxiously in bed when she returned, his face turned towards the bright rectangle of the doorway.

"Yes, father. I have just been down to the creek to bathe. It is still early. I will get some breakfast."

The blind knight nodded and lay down again. He felt easier now that his daughter was with him. His visual world was made up of diffuse shapes and patterns, flashes of light and darkness, and very little else. Each day even this paltry remnant of his sight seemed to grow dimmer. Last night the much-touted Wall had appeared to him only as a marginally brighter portion of his fading universe. Yet he had listened carefully to Donella's description. *"It is like a great fiery window in the sky, father."* He could tell from the way she spoke that the apparition frightened her. While he had lost most of his vision, he had gained a deep understanding of the subtle nuances of speech. His daughter had had much practice in 'seeing' for him, and while he listened to her he carefully built in his mind an image of the valley, of The Wall, and the number of monks and pilgrims settled nearby. This gave him much to ponder upon, and explained to some extent his restless sleep.

"How are you feeling this morning?" Donella asked.

He could hear her making the familiar sounds of breakfast preparations: rattling cups and other utensils as she dipped into their meagre supplies.

42

"Well enough, lass. And you?"

"I was up at first-light. The morning is cool and beautiful, father. But of The Wall there is scarcely a sign."

Just then the old shepherd stirred on his bed of straw, rolled over, yawned and sat up.

Donella said, "Good morning, Angus Mallory. I am just preparing breakfast, We do not have much. Some dark bread, a little cheese and sausage. . ."

Mallory rubbed his eyes, grunted, and stood up, keeping his blanket wrapped around him; his old bones disliked the morning air as much as the evening. "I have gruel," he said, "if that be to your liking. And herb tea."

Donella smiled at the old man. "You are most generous."

Outside the first rays of sunlight pierced the valley. Pilgrims, and others who had spent their night in the open were getting up and about, exercising their cramped limbs and preparing their simple breakfasts.

The Wall was gossamer-thin above the lake, but clearly visible now that the sun had touched it. It looked like an enormous silver web which had been spun overnight by a legion of busy fairies. Donella smiled wryly to herself for conjuring up such an image.

Yet it would soon change.

●　●　●

Conrad and his Master had hardly slept at all. The monks had begun their matins at midnight, chanting with a fervour that kept the two Scientists awake until dawn, at which time the worthy brothers had retired for a short nap before taking up their tasks for the day.

Usually matins consisted of one brisk chant, three anthems, three psalms and three lessons, plus a few extra celebrations on various saints' days. But late last night the Abbot had come hurrying down from his eyrie, and, with a burst of fanatical zeal, had himself led the hapless monks through a marathon performance of fifty-three psalms, a

43

feat of inspired devotion and energy that must have pleased all Heaven and put the Devil in a foul mood for the rest of the day. This excess of devotion had been inspired by the splendour of The Wall. . . and perhaps by the Abbot's earnest desire to expiate his sins.

No breakfast was served to the weary monks. Their order dined only once daily, at noon—except on special days, when a light supper was permitted. But Asquith's generous contribution to the monastery's dwindling coffers ensured that he and Conrad, at least, enjoyed a hearty breakfast: fresh bread, a little wine, eggs and beans.

Conrad eyed the wine dubiously. Asquith smiled across the table. "Come on, lad, get a drop of it into you. But slowly: it helps the digestion. The food will soak it up well enough, and if you slept as ill as myself, then it may help to sweep the cobwebs from your head."

The boy took this advice. He did not experience the promised consolation at once, but the dark red wine was pleasant enough and went well with the food.

The morning was well advanced when they mounted and set out from the monastery: The Wall shone clearly now with a cool, golden light, reflecting the newly risen sun. It was not yet bright enough to dazzle curious onlookers, many of whom had moved close to the shore of the lake to get a better look at the phenomenon. Later in the day conditions would not be so suitable for such close scrutiny. . . or scientific investigation.

Asquith rode towards the northern side of the valley, where he intended to approach The Wall edge-on and get some idea of its thickness, among other things. Conrad carried several sharpened sticks across his saddle. These would be driven into the ground to mark the farthest extent of The Wall on either side of the valley, and also to indicate the present shoreline of the lake. Then on the morrow they would be able to measure any significant growth in either aspect of the phenomenon. The prospect of their investigation filled the boy with excitement.

He noted some activity in the valley. Although it was still early, a steady stream of newcomers was already weaving down the narrow path. Even at this distance he could distinguish travelling hucksters, their carts heavily laden with a variety of wares and foodstuffs. The first few stalls would soon set up by people eager to exploit the situation: the pungent odours of freshly cooked meat and vegetables would mingle with those of wine and ale.

"This looks like becoming a fete," he remarked casually.

Asquith nodded grimly. It was no more than he had expected. And there would be worse to come.

The northern slope was steep. They proceeded cautiously downhill, their horses picking their way carefully over the uneven ground. Soon they were close enough to the diffused edge of The Wall to see how its brightness faded away at this point. At its central area, directly above the lake, Asquith guessed that the drops of water were closer together; this would explain the relative difference in brightness. It was like a solid mass of sunlight in the centre of the valley, but up here it faded away into a tenuous curtain of moisture, still shimmering faintly in the sunlight.

Asquith dismounted only a short distance from the edge of the phenomenon. He stood in silence for a few minutes, deep in thought. "This is how it must have looked to the old man when he first saw it," he said eventually. "How did he put it? *'Like a bit o' dew dangling in the air.'* "

Conrad dismounted and joined his Master. Together they stepped closer to the curtain of moisture. Seen so close, the individual drops sparkled brilliantly, liked tiny jewels. To their left, The Wall swept away and condensed into its solid-seeming centre above the lake.

He followed Asquith a short distance uphill, until they came to a spot where there were no visible signs of moisture in the air.

"Here, lad. Drive a marker *there*"—Asquith indicated the

spot with a wave of his hand. Conrad hurried back to where his mount was cropping disinterestedly at the stunted grass, withdrew one of the sharpened sticks from the bundle strapped to his saddle, and hurried back. Following Asquith's guidance, he drove the stick deeply into the hard soil. It was not easy; the ground was hard and he had first to dig with his dagger, then come down heavily on the stick to wedge it tight. When this was done to his Master's satisfaction, the boy looked up.

"Good," Asquith said, testing the rigidity of the marker.

While his Master made sure the marker was secure, the boy wandered downhill to take a closer look at the droplets of water suspended in the air. On impulse he reached out and swept his right hand boldly through them, collecting some moisture on his fingertips and in his palm.

He tasted the moisture as carefully as he had tasted the lake water. He looked up and called out: "It is pure, Master. No trace of salt."

Yet a chill had penetrated the hand he swept through the moisture. He shivered, for no reason he could understand.

Asquith came down to where he stood. He stared at the shimmering dew. "Hm. I wonder how it would taste farther down?"

But Conrad wasn't listening. He was staring down at his hand, fascinated. The chill had retreated to his fingers now. Then to his fingertips. . . it was gone.

But had it really been there! he wondered, or had he only imagined it? A strange chill, like nothing he had ever felt before.

"Come", Asquith said. "We have some hard riding ahead of us."

When they reached the rim of the valley and paused to look behind them, they were both astounded to discover how thin The Wall appeared. At no point—not even at the central section above the lake—did it seem more than a fraction of an inch through. In fact, no denser than a single drop of dew.

"Extraordinary!" Asquith exclaimed. Then his eyes narrowed and he pointed with his right hand. "And mark you now, the *curvature.*"

Conrad nodded. There could be no mistaking his Master's observation: The Wall did curve outwards slightly, towards the western side of the valley. This curvature was no more than a few degrees, but it was worth noting. Both made sure the fact was entered into their record books before they proceeded with their Investigation.

The monks, they saw, were busily engaged in erecting some sort of wooden platform near the shore of the lake. It was too early to imagine what they intended to do with it, but they did not doubt it was part of some devious plan of the Abbot's devising.

"Perhaps they plan to sail it," Asquith said, and laughed. "Sail it across the lake and take a close look at The Wall for themselves."

Conrad doubted this. It was not in the monks' nature to question any vision openly.

They rode on, making their way around the western rim of the valley. Here they discovered something even more unusual. As they moved around *behind* The Wall, they were astonished to see it disappear! The eastern side of the valley was as clear to them as the land directly below. And yet, not quite so clear. . .

When they realized that they were looking *through* The Wall, certain disparities became evident. The eastern side of the valley seemed somewhat more brightly lit than the western slopes; this would be in accordance with the sunlight being reflected from the opposite face of The Wall. But it was Conrad who first noticed the subtle distortions. The distant human figures, their stalls and tents and the hard-working monks by the water's edge—all appeared strangely elongated.

Why, it is just like looking through a lens! the boy realized. Jubilant, he said as much to his Master.

47

Asquith narrowed his eyes. "Aye, you seem to be on the right track, sure enough. This thing must be some kind of membrane, then, stretched out across the valley—reflecting the sunlight from one side, and allowing light to pass through the other. Tell me, lad", —he turned to Conrad—"Did you feel any resistance when you passed your hand through the moisture?"

The boy hesitated. All he remembered was the uncanny chill, but that had quickly passed. "No, I recall no resistance, sir."

"Hm. Well, we'll make a better test when we reach the other side."

They rode on, intrigued by the faintly distorted picture they were getting of the activity in the valley.

When they reached the southernmost edge of The Wall they again dismounted, and, under Master Asquith's watchful eye, Conrad once more passed his hand through the tenuous arm of the phenomenon.

He experienced a moment of surprise, as before, when he first plunged his hand through the mist; and his expression did not pass unnoticed by his Master.

"Keep it there a moment," Asquith said, stepping closer. "Tell me if you feel anything. . . anything at all."

Already Conrad could feel the chill working its way through his fingers and up his arm. Already it was past his elbow, and—

"Sir!"

"Yes?"

"I feel a strange chill. I felt it back there, but only for a moment." He was holding his arm out rigid, so that his hand was on the other side of The Wall. "It . . . I can feel it moving up my arm. I can feel it in my shoulder . . ."

He could feel it creeping down towards his heart, up towards his brain, towards the seat of his reason. He grew afraid. "Sir!"

Asquith gave a deep sigh. "Step back, lad. Let me

see. . ."

So grateful was Conrad for the sudden reprieve that he almost stumbled backwards and nearly lost his footing. He stood massaging his chilled arm vigorously while he watched Asquith duplicate his action.

The older man stood quite still for several minutes with his hand outstretched, passing it through the mist. Except for a growing concentration there was nothing in his expression to indicate that he shared the student's feelings. Then he stood back abruptly, looked down at his arm with a puzzled frown, and began massaging it promptly. He turned around and stared rather foolishly at Conrad, who by now had regained most of his former confidence; there was only a tingle in his fingertips to remind him of the cold terror that had gripped him.

"Indeed you are right, lad," his Master agree. "It is like plunging one's hand into icy water. But the most extraordinary feature is the fact that this area of intense cold is so narrow. *No wider than a drop of water.* —Did you detect any substance other than water: any membrane or such that might explain how this dew accumulates and how The Wall is able to act like a lens?"

Conrad could only shake his head. "No sir. There was only . . . the cold." His sleeve was quite wet; it had sopped up considerable moisture.

Asquith gave a deep sigh. He had finished massaging life back into his own arm and was once more considering the baffling nature of this mystery. "Still, the cold was so intense that it might have blocked off any other sensation. You agree?"

Conrad thought this a reasonable supposition. It was entered into their record books. Then Conrad drove another marker into the hard ground and they rode off.

●   ●   ●

As they descended again into the valley, The Wall greeted

them with its vivid new face: it was now close to noon and from this aspect the phenomenon had begun to reflect the sunlight with its customary intensity. An odd mixture of sounds drifted up to them: people talking among themselves, hucksters crying their wares. A column of dust hung over the narrow path leading down into the valley, where a constant stream of newcomers wound their way on foot and horse-back or in rickety old carts pulled by oxen.

"They seemed determined to make a fair out of this," the boy observed.

"Aye, that they do. I wonder what your Abbot thinks about it all". Asquith knew the Abbot would disapprove of such activities, but there seemed precious little he or the monks could do about it.

"What do you think the monks are building?" the boy said presently.

Asquith shrugged. "Some sort of shrine, I expect. Where the devout may worship in peace, far from that motley crowd. I will allow that there are precious few genuine pilgrims among that lot."

Mallory's house was on their right now. But all the boy could see were a few scraggy head of sheep grazing down by the creek. He wondered if the knight, his daughter and their bodyguard had departed, and why such a thought should disturb him.

Asquith led him to the water's edge, some distance from where the monks laboured, so that they might inspect the lake in peace. They dismounted and stepped forward. The Master squatted on his haunches and dabbled his fingers in the cool water. It was surprisingly clear. He ran the tip of his tongue over his wet fingers and pulled a wry face.

"Arrh, indeed you were right enough, Conrad; this water is too salty for my liking. Strange. . ."

Before them the lake shimmered brightly, reflecting the brilliance of The Wall overhead.

Asquith waded out a few yards and peered into the water.

50

He seemed to be looking for something, some vital clue, perhaps, that would enable them to unravel this mystery. Or so the student hoped. His Master's patience was, to him, a constant source of wonder, yet he knew that it was only through such patience that the unknown might at last be understood.

As Conrad waited by the shore, he darted quick glances in the direction of the old shepherd's house; once he thought he spied the girl, Donella, standing in the doorway, watching them. But when he looked again she was gone.

"Conrad!"

Quickly the boy snapped his attention back to the work in hand.

"Come here, lad . . ."

Conrad waded out to join his Master, ignoring the strange looks they were beginning to get from some monks nearest to them.

They stood together. "We need samples of this water," Asquith explained, "so that it can be examined at the College. And for that purpose we need bottles, flasks, flagons—anything that will serve as a container and not be sullied."

"Then we must have glass," the boy said quickly.

"Aye. But good earthenware will do in a pinch. Where do you think we could possibly find good flasks in this outlandish place, eh?"

"Flagons we should find a-plenty in Pietro's tavern," Conrad said. "And I did hear of a local apothecary at Northbridge. He will surely have some spare flasks."

Asquith clapped a warm arm around his shoulder. "Good thinking, lad. I had forgotten all about the apothecary. We must seek him out and see if we can tease some of his treasures from him with jingling coin, eh?"

They waded back to the shore. The boy directed a stern gaze at the hard-working monks. "Would that they worked so conscientiously for the truth, Master Asquith."

51

The Scientist shook his head in a chiding gesture. "Do not waste your thoughts on them, Conrad. Look yonder: see the number of stalls already set up by greedy traders eager to relieve pious pilgrims of their money! Tomorrow there will be twice as many again, and the day after that. . ." He shuddered. "That I prefer not to think about. Too many people can only hinder our Investigation."

The vanguard would consist of the usual wandering bands of pilgrims and other religious zealots. In time their numbers would be swollen by the merely curious as well as the devout—as indeed they were already—and these would be joined by weary knights and their attendants. They would be followed by the sceptical, the disenchanted, the jaded, the indolent, the lonely, the spiritually bankrupt. Among them would be found the usual sprinkling of rogues and vagabonds and whores eager to extract an easy penny. Only a handful would come seeking their private truths, some to recapture discarded dreams—oh, there would be pranksters and parasites a–plenty ready to deceive the unwise and unwary. What a tawdry enterprise they would be forced to witness!

"Come on, lad," Asquith said. "Let us get off to Northbridge while the day is still young and before the highway becomes choked with sightseers."

Behind them The Wall burned brighter every moment, a blazing beacon now known throughout the land, drawing people to it like moths to a flame.

A knight of the realm

"What are they doing now, Donella?"

All morning she had kept watch in the doorway of Mallory's house, describing to her father the busy monks and marking the new arrivals who made their way into the valley. Often she heard him shuffling across the stone floor and, moments later, feel the gentle pressure of his hand upon her shoulder as he leaned against the door jamb. She felt his presence now, and knew that his useless eyes would be looking blindly in the general direction of the lake.

More than an hour had passed since she had first spied the two horsemen on the far side of the valley. They were so far away from every other activity that she sensed immediately it must be the Scientist, Roger Asquith, and his young apprentice. She had watched them make their way down the steep northern slope to where that arm of The Wall ended, saw them dismount and linger for a while, then ride on around the western rim of the valley until they reached the other arm of the phenomenon, where their business was repeated. This time they were closer and she could observe their activities in more detail. She was puzzled, and described what was happening to her father, who found the whole business passing strange. She saw the boy—Conrad—drive some sort of marker into the ground. Then they remounted as before and made their way slowly down into the valley.

They rode towards the lake, dismounting at the shore, with some distance between them and the busy monks. She thought there was something calculated and purposeful in

their movements which set them apart from the general air of festivity that appeared to have overtaken the valley. Snatches of her conversation with Conrad came drifting back to her, and she marvelled at the dedication that drove him on in the face of such a mystery.

She saw the older man kneel down by the water's edge and paddle his fingers in the lake. The younger stood waiting, a few paces back. Fragments of their conversation came drifting across to her, but she could make no sense out of them.

"Donella?" Again, the urgent pressure on her shoulder. "They are wading out into the lake," she said. "They appear to be studying the water."

Her father made a gruff noise. "And what do they expect to find, I wonder?"

She considered this for a moment. Then, grown bold with the responsibility thrust upon her she said, "Shall I go and ask them? It is but a short distance—a few hundred yards, no more."

"A moment." Her father grasped her shoulder rather roughly, which he was wont to do whenever he was concentrating. Then his grip relaxed. "Aye, go—and ask them back for a simple repast. I have a mind to meet with and talk to these men who call themselves 'Scientists'.—Hakim!"

Donella touched her father gently on the cheek. "I will have no need of Hakim. Let him stay here to watch over you. It is but a short walk to the lake, and the two Scientists have swords to protect me."

"Nonetheless," he said grimly, "Hakim will keep a watch out for you. Do not dally with them, Donella, if they decline to eat with us. But give them my greeting, for they seem to be men of uncommon good sense."

Without another word, Donella set off towards the lake.

● ● ●

Another hour and it would be noon. Already The Wall glowed brilliantly, once again like a surface of polished

56

metal reflecting the sunlight. The figures of the Scientist and his apprentice were tiny silhouettes dwarfed by the phenomenon they had chosen to study. Far away to their right the worthy brothers of the monastery of St Germaine continued their industrious work. A fresh load of timber had just been dumped from an ox-cart and they were busy sorting it out.

The two Scientists were so deeply engaged in conversation that they did not hear the girl approach. She made a point of treading heavily on the ground and humming softly to herself when she was but a short distance away.

They both turned around, momentarily caught off-guard.

The boy spoke first. "Good morning, Donella."

Standing so close to The Wall, she had to shield her eyes from the brightness in order to see him clearly. His face was pleasant enough, she decided, but his features were soft, not well-graven enough to be called handsome.

"Good morning, Conrad," she replied. "I have been watching your movements for some time, and also the labours of those poor wretches yonder." She nodded in the direction of the busy monks. "My father and I are curious to know what you are about."

The boy drew himself up so that he seemed even taller than before. "Donella, we have not come here to worship this thing, but to study it. To unlock its mysteries, if we can. That is why we have been so busy this morning."

She inclined her head a little to one side and gave him a keen look. "You talk like a book," she said. "Tell me what you *know*."

Asquith, who had been on the verge of entering into the conversation, smiled to himself and kept silent. Let the young ones work it out between them. . .

Her words had taken the wind out of the student; he needed a moment to regain his composure. "I. . . I know what I have learned, that is for sure. I give no credence to myth and folk-tale—"

57

"Aye, it seems you know well enough what you have been *told*". The lass, standing with her hands on her hips and her head held high, obviously relished a good argument. Then she remembered the reason for her calling on these men, and courtesy took over. "My father has asked me to request your company for a simple meal, if this be to your liking. As a knight of the realm who has fought far and wide across the world, he is a well-educated man who desires to hear something of your studies."

Asquith smiled warmly. "Why, lass, we would be delighted to accept your offer. But we can stay only a short while: we have business in Northbridge that will not wait too long."

She nodded. "My father will understand."

Asquith remounted and turned his horse towards the house. "Come now, Donella," he said, "get up behind the boy. No sense in you walking all the way back while we ride in comfort." His expression carried a mild rebuke for Conrad, because he had not thought of this himself.

Conrad said nothing. He leaned over and helped the girl up and behind him. His face was expressionless. "Hold on to me," he said.

Her arms grasped his waist as they moved off. But for some reason her grip was hesitant; instead of holding his body firmly, her arms hung loosely around him. He made no comment. Several times the jolting of the horse threw her gently forward, so that her small breasts pressed for a moment against his firm back. The contact sent a tremor passing through her.

Hakim was at his post outside the doorway. He gave a crooked expression that passed for a smile when they arrived. Donella quickly disengaged herself from the boy and jumped to the ground.

"Good day, Hakim," Asquith said, doffing his hat and offering a smile. The giant nodded, making of the gesture something close to a bow. Then he motioned them inside.

The blind knight was standing beside the table, resting his right hand upon it for support and looking in the general direction of the open doorway. He saw vague shadows move through an area of brightness and knew that his guests were standing before him. Had he stood upright he would have been a good head taller than Asquith, but the burden of time and war had given him a permanent stoop. The old shepherd was away from home, tending his sparse flock.

Donella moved quickly to her father's side, placing a gentle hand upon his arm. "They have come, father," she whispered.

"Aye, that I know, lass," he answered in an equally soft voice. Then he addressed his visitors. "Welcome, gentlemen! Donella has told me much about you; indeed, so much that I feel a strong desire to talk to you. As you observe, I am blind, or very nearly so. So you will please forgive an old soldier if his manner does not always seem attentive." He tapped his left ear. "But whatever my eyes signal, let me assure you that my ears will give you the whole of my attention. Let me introduce myself: I am Ramon de Vargas, knight of the realm; my daughter you already know, also Hakim, my squire, who keeps watch outside. Had it not been for the Saracen I would never have returned home; worms would be feeding off my frozen carcase in those icy northlands. But enough of the past. Sit down, good sirs."

He held out his hand in welcome. Asquith stepped forward and grasped it firmly. "I am Roger Asquith," he said, "and I am proud to meet both you and your daughter—and your loyal squire." He motioned to Conrad to come forward. "This is the hand of my apprentice, Conrad le Jeune."

The boy almost winced when the blind knight's hand closed around his, his grasp was so strong. "It is not often," he said, "that we meet one as well-travelled as yourself."

A dark cloud seemed to pass suddenly across de Vargas' scarred visage. "Aye, surely I am—'well travelled', lad." And he laughed, as though at some private joke. "Donella

59

has told me much about your activities," he went on. He felt his way around the edge of the table until he came up against the stool; then he sat down, his hands clasped before him on the table.

His daughter took up a position on his left, her hand upon his shoulder. For a moment her eyes strayed in the direction of the boy. His face was flushed and he avoided her eyes. She wondered if this was because he felt awkward in the commanding presence of her father, or whether . . . She felt the blood rush suddenly to her own face when she recalled how her arms had linked themselves reluctantly about him and how her breasts had pressed against his back. Even now her body tingled from the memory; she found that she, too, could not meet his gaze. Instead, she looked down while her father spoke.

The blind knight raised one hand and passed it briefly across his ruined face. "You must understand," he said, "that I was not always as you see me now—as my daughter can well testify. I was once as devout a knight as you might find anywhere in this realm; I could still dispute with yonder Abbot and his underlings the finer points of the gospels. It was held by many that I was learned in such matters. But this was many years ago, you understand, when knighthood was a demanding occupation, not the brawling, wining, wenching business it has since become. Some say this is because of the wars. I say it is the general fault of the times.—Why, I can recall as if it were yesterday how I would rise before sun-up and stay and prayer for at least two hours. And I heard—on my knees, mark you—a Mass every day, sometimes two. On Fridays I always dressed in black. On Sundays and festal days I would make pilgrimage on foot, or discourse on holy matters with my fellow knights, or have someone read to me the life of one of our illustrious saints. We spoke scarcely at all, and when we did it was mostly about God and His scriptures. In this way did I become a knight of Albion, gentlemen, and carry His word both near

60

and far. Aye, and carried His war as well, when that mad prophet in the frozen North sent his heathen hordes against the Holy City of Athens.''

Asquith and the boy stood quite still while they heard the blind knight out. It was obviously an oft-told tale, but simple courtesy and a respect for de Vargas' suffering restrained them from growing restless.

The knight's voice grew increasingly bitter as his story progressed. Once he even spat angrily at the floor when he recalled a flood of memories he usually kept hidden. His dark eyes narrowed. ''It was a bloody war we fought. And had it not been for our allies surging up from the burning lands to the south—why, even now the See of Adrian would be destroyed and those heathens would occupy the holiest of all cities.'' His scarred face managed a hideous grin. ''Aye, we fought ice with fire, the fiery passion of the Saracens. Those hot lands breed warriors such as I have never seen the likes of, gentlemen. And slowly we drove the heathen back out of Greece, sometimes losing a little ground, but mostly gaining. The farther we drove them back the more terrible the land became. Often I wondered what sort of creature could live in such an inhospitable clime, yet I well know that our friendly neighbours in Denmark and Sweden somehow manage to wrest a living from the soil. But this was worse, far worse. People, wriggling like lice, trying to drag some life from the frozen ground. And there was a madness in their eyes, a madness any false prophet could have seized upon were the moment ripe. Perhaps we were all a little mad. And have I not heard, only recently, that the heathen hordes are once again on the march, and that yet another Crusade has been launched to drive them back?''

Asquith nodded: ''Aye, that is so. At this very moment, I hear, the Slavs have captured most of Italy, and almost cut off all help from our quarter. You are right in this respect: they are indeed insane, with a quality of madness that enables men to overcome monstrous odds.''

Ramon de Vargas nodded sadly. "This time the burden will fall heavily on our allies, the Saracens, to protect the Holy City. But I have been given to understand that Spain, my native country, is even now putting together a mighty armada of ships which it intends to sail through the Mediterranean, to strike at the very heel of Italy and carry the war on from there.—Ah, but I grow weary of such talk." The old man held his head in his hands and muttered: "Men will find ways of making war until the end of time, of that I am convinced. Of that, and no more."

He lifted his head and stared at them with his blind eyes. "For five long years I fought a bloody war, gentlemen, and nowhere did I find any sign of His divine presence. Instead, I bore witness to such sights that should have curdled my reason. I have waded through the dead piled so high you could not see the sun at noon; in many a heathen temple I have seen my countrymen riding in blood up to their stirrups. And often have I asked myself: was it for *this* God gave me eyes? And it was almost as if in answer to my constant questioning that he took my sight from me. Well, so be it. I must have offended Him greatly with my nagging!" de Vargas gave a hollow laugh.

"In time I found my way back to my homeland, thanks to Hakim's tender care. And what did I find?" His voice rose and he pounded a fist on the table. "My castle taken from me! My wife . . . *murdered.* My estate in the hands of robber barons who smirked and shook a document across my face-that had been signed with the name of our mad King!" His voice shook; his body trembled, but he went on. He reached out and grasped his daughter's hand with intense affection. "There remained some old friends—good people, all of them— who saw my wretched state and helped me to find my daughter, my fair Donella. . . working as a common serving-wench in an ale house!"

Donella bit her lip so hard that a trickle of blood flowed. She glanced up; there, on the other side of the table, was the boy Scientist looking directly at her. Their eyes met. And this time no flush came to either of their cheeks, although the girl felt her body tremble. She wanted desperately to close her eyes, to blot out everything, but she knew this was impossible. After a moment the boy looked away, perhaps sensing her need to be left alone.

The Knight's voice dropped and he brooded over his hands. "Now they say there is a 'miracle' in this valley. From what Donella has told me, and since so many people have journeyed here, it seems a likely proposition. And yet, I wonder if it is by some jest of His that I am brought here— to be made aware, at last, of a sign of His presence when I am no longer capable of seeing anything, and must rely instead upon another's eyes?"

His chest was rising and falling rapidly as his breathing grew erratic. "Gently, father," Donella murmured.

The knight's voice dropped and be brooded over his again his voice was calm. "My daughter says you call yourself Scientists. Does that mean you have come to disprove this 'miracle'?"

Asquith was wary of how he should reply. He held up a hand to restrain Conrad from jumping into the breach without thinking. The gesture was not lost upon the girl.

"The land is rife with many a false tale," he said, "as you yourself well know."

de Vargas nodded. "Donella, fetch our visitors some bread and wine while we talk."

Asquith thanked the knight for his courtesy; and it was in the friendly atmosphere of a group of acquaintances sharing a meal together that the Master Scientist explained his position.

"We are students of nature, sir knight, and it is through our study of nature that we become, ultimately, students of God—for does not the Being Whom we call God manifest Himself in every living thing—perhaps in every object?"

The blind knight nodded sagaciously, downing a quantity

of dark-red wine. "Aye, that sounds reasonable enough."

"You have called yourself a learned man, Ramon de Vargas, and have given us ample evidence that you are. Yet the Church distrusts our motives; it would rather men should remain ignorant of nature and be shackled with superstition, the better to exploit them for the Church's own ends. What use are so many fine churches throughout the land when so many of our people are starving? Can this truly be His divine wish? I think not. The Church persecutes our activities and charges our members with all sorts of imaginary crimes. They will not accept that a religion can be based upon a true and proper knowledge of the world, such as we seek to discover, instead of ignorance and superstition."

"And how long do you expect it will take, this study you speak of?"

"Why, it will take ages, my lord! Nature is too vast to be taken in and understood by a handful of dedicated men, all in the space of one short lifetime! We work not only for today, but for the limitless future."

de Vargas uttered a deep sigh. "Noble sentiments, gentlemen. And nobly expressed, Roger Asquith. I can see that the shedding of some fresh light of wisdom on our world might make it a better place to live in. Certainly the old ways have brought us nothing but suffering and hardship. It is as though our lives are in ill-worked patchwork, the whole adding up to. . . nothing." He sat quite still, a broken figure of a man with his head in his hands.

The girl said softly, "My father is not well. He suffers a great pain every now and again. So much talk has exhausted him."

"Yet he spoke courageously and well," Asquith replied. "It is not every day one meets with one who has fought and travelled so widely those stark northern wastes."

They finished their luncheon and bid their farewells. "We have business in Northbridge," Asquith explained," that cannot wait. Thank you for your hospitality." He bowed to the girl. Conrad merely nodded.

The blind knight lifted his head, squinting at the dark blurs set against the brightness he knew to be the doorway. "What business, if I might be so bold as to ask, sir?"

"We need some flasks and stone flagons to take samples of the lake water," the Scientist explained. "We intend to seek a local apothecary. He should be able to help us out with a spare flask or two."

de Vargas nodded. "Aye—and the innkeeper should have more than enough stone flagons for your purpose—that is, unless you plan to drain yonder lake." He laughed ruefully at his joke. "God speed you, then. I would consider it an honour if you would return from time to time, so that I may be kept informed of your progress."

"We will keep in touch," Asquith promised. Not only had he come to regard the tragic figure of the knight and his fair daughter with a sense of friendship, but it crossed his mind that the shepherd's house would serve as an ideal base from which to conduct their Investigation, well away from the watchful eye of the Abbot.

A puzzled frown crossed de Vargas' face. "You have not told me," he said, "Where you are staying."

The boy could not resist a smile when he answered, "Why, at the monastery, Sir."

"The *monastery?* But surely—"

"Where else?" Asquith quipped. "With that rabble in the valley? No, we are safe and well enough disguised to move safely within the camp of our enemies—if they be such. Not all Churchmen are hostile to our cause, but their numbers are precious few. Yet in time that, too, might change. Farewell, for the time being, sir knight. We shall keep you informed, never fear."

Donella saw them outside. "Thank you," she said, "For giving up so much of your time."

"It is nothing, lass," Asquith said, climbing into the saddle. "And we will keep our promise and return, when we

65

have got on with our work.''

She turned around to go back inside and found herself facing the boy. His face was stern; she had seen that expression before, and wondered what it was he took so much trouble to withhold. Her mind filled with the tactile memory of his broad back pressing against her breasts. She smiled and said, ''Goodbye, Conrad.''

He muttered something she did not hear, gave a stiff bow, and quickly remounted. Their glances locked briefly while he was in the saddle; for a moment he seemed to be looking not at but into her. Then he rode away.

She raised one hand to a burning cheek, feeling a wave of dizziness wash over her for a moment. For she had begun to realize that the boy's seemingly sullen silences concealed unknown depths. Shaken, she made her way back inside the house.

●　　●　　●

The two Scientists rode in a wide arc that took them well clear of the tawdry township with its bustle and noise. They passed close by the toiling monks, and now they recognized the construction as a dais: already the monks were beginning to overlay the wooden platform with the first long spokes of a Wheel.

Conrad noticed this only vaguely. Another vision now burned so brightly in his mind that for a while it outshone the splendour of The Wall. It was the face of the girl, Donella. A ragged little urchin no man would have called pretty, for at some time in the past mere prettiness had been taken from her. Yet this tragic aspect of her character gave her a dignity and bearing uncommon for her age. No, she was not pretty.

He thought her most beautiful.

SIX

The face in the flask

The road to Northbridge teemed with travellers. Most trudged wearily on foot, travel-stained, with glum faces, for they had not yet seen the miracle they had come so far to witness. A few were on horseback, a goodly number of them knights, some weighed down with costly armour, others wearing chain-mail in need of repair. Tumbrils bounced and jogged along the uneven surface. Dust hung heavily in the air; it was difficult to breathe.

"Soon this flow of sightseers will have swollen into an army," Asquith muttered darkly.

Conrad said nothing. His mind was still enamoured of its new-found muse. He rode with his head down, letting his mare find her own way.

"Something troubling you, lad?" Asquith inquired.

The boy looked up for a moment, startled, like one roused suddenly from a dream.

Asquith gave an understanding smile. "I'll wager it's the lass back there who has drowsed your soul, eh?"

Conrad nodded and gave a rueful grin. He felt a trifle guilty, as though he had been caught out in some minor misdemeanour. "Aye, she is a strange one, all right."

His Master grew stern. Looking straight ahead he remarked, almost casually, "I think that is because she was made a woman ere she was finished with being a child." He left this cryptic statement hanging in the air, then said: "Remember, we have urgent business to attend to, Conrad. Do not let her beauty cloud your thoughts for long."

67

The boy's heart took a wild leap. That his Master had also recognized Donella's unique beauty made him feel almost lightheaded.

They rode on past the motley cavalcade in silence.

●　　●　　●

Northbridge was bustling with activity when they arrived. The streets were crowded with more people than there had been in decades as pilgrims and adventurers poured in from all over the land.

Pietro's tavern had enjoyed a roaring trade for a while, but his supplies of ale soon ran out. He had sent agents scurrying to the monastery for fresh casks, but his men returned looking puzzled, complaining that the monks had agreed that they could have all the ale they required, and at the usual price, but that Pietro must supply them with his own empty casks, for the worthy brothers had none to spare.

Pietro thought this rather strange. But when he considered that the Abbot had not hoisted his prices—as he himself already had, to take advantage of the increase in trade—he was ready enough to go along with the unusual request. "Break out all the empty casks we have!" he bellowed. "And when you've done that, see what can be done about getting more made!" For they must have ale; the travellers demanded it. Already they were grumbling over his sour wines which they were forced to drink. "A little patience," he begged of them, "and you will soon have all the ale you need!" Meantime he sweated copiously and hoped he could maintain the even temper of the crowd while his servants hurried back to the monastery.

The two Scientists were passing by the tavern when all this was going on. Asquith smiled. "It seems that our jolly host of yesternight did not anticipate such a great influx of customers!"

Asquith's right hand, Conrad noticed, never strayed far from the hilt of his sword. His Master also kept a sharp eye on the people surging around them, knowing well the shifty movements of thieves and cutpurses and the like which they could expect among this cross-section of humanity, the inevitable parasites that accompanied any venture of this sort.

" 'Twould be wise to watch our words while we are here," he warned quietly. "I like not the temper of some I have seen. And keep an eye on thy purse."

The boy nodded grimly. He, too, had been disturbed by some of the faces he had seen in the crowd. In fact, very few of the people seemed to have come here intent to witness a miracle; their thoughts seemed more turned towards mischief than worship. And there would be worse to come; this was but the vanguard. Master Asquith was continually impressing this upon him. Conrad's heart gave a wrench when he thought of Mallory and the human pestilence about to descend upon his beloved valley.

Asquith selected carefully from among the throng before he paused to ask a question. With uncanny skill he chose one of the older and less harried women who appeared to be a resident of Northbridge. "Tell me, good lady," he said, bowing from his saddle, "where might I find the local apothecary?"

She squinted up at him, paused for a moment, then pointed back down the street. "Down the end there, last house on the left."

"Thank you, my good woman," he said. And set off down the street with Conrad.

They dismounted outside a tumbledown dwelling and hitched their horses to a nearby stump. Asquith gave a quick look around, then knocked heavily upon the wooden door that seemed the most solid part of the house.

A moment later the door was opened by the most ancient man Conrad had ever seen. He wore a long grey cassock marked with grime and faded, arcane symbols. His grizzled beard came down past his waist. His head was quite bald, the flesh all shrivelled on his face. He gazed at them through watery eyes.

Asquith quickly got to the point; he asked the old man if he had some flasks and vials to spare, "If possible, we desire the very best Spanish glass," he added.

The apothecary mumbled and procrastinated and kept the door only half-open. The jingle of silver coins in Asquith's outstretched palm soon won him over.

"Come in, then," he grumbled. "I'll see what I can find."

Inside, the house was festooned with cobwebs and layered over with dust. Heavy tomes were scattered here and there, some stacked in piles, others left open. The boy's eyes widened with delight: how he would have liked to have spent a few hours among those books! For it was well known that many a secret of nature which the Church had suppressed could be rediscovered in the ancient writings of the great alchemists. Some of his excitement must have been evident in his expression, for Asquith placed a restraining hand upon his arm. "Curb thy enthusiasm, Conrad. There will be other times. . . and more old men such as he. And plenty of great books to discover."

The apothecary disappeared up a ramshackle staircase; they could hear him muddling around overhead. A small shower of dust descended from the ceiling, shaken free by so much activity. Master and student smiled at each other; it helped to ease the tension.

"These will have to do," the old man mumbled, reappearing. In his wrinkled hands he held two slender phials and two medium-sized flasks, all made from the finest glass and with cork stoppers.

"Oh, well done, apothecary!" Asquith cried, scarcely able to believe their good fortune. He took the proffered flasks and passed the delicate phials into Conrad's care. The silver coins he doled out brought a gleam into the old man's eyes that had probably not been present for a quarter of a century. Asquith, for his part, considered he had bought

70

himself a bargain.

As they were about to leave, a spirit of comradeship encouraged the Scientist to confide in the old man—for were not his kind as persecuted by the Church as they? "Listen, old man, it would seem that you, like this village, have fallen on hard times. Mark you this: Pietro and his tavern have been doing a roaring trade and are constantly running short of supplies. Surely you can carve yourself a slice of this business? I have heard tell that a wise apothecary can distill the most fiery spirits from his apparatus! Hundreds more have yet to arrive here, probably thousands. It would be to your advantage to be prepared."

As they rode off, the old man was left with a mixture of puzzlement and cunning on his face. He waved after them and thanked them. Then he hurried back inside.

●　●　●

They wasted no more time in Northbridge but rode straight back to the valley. By now it was well past noon and the sun had begun to slide down from its low autumn meridian. A sharp wind had risen in the north; it had stirred up the clouds and scattered them willy-nilly across the sky. Today's sunset promised to be even more spectacular than before. Already The Wall was blazing fiercely as it built up gradually towards an overwhelming splendour.

They found the entrance into the valley choked with a great number of poor people who had come to gaze rapturously upon the miracle, but who had neither the means nor the intention of remaining overnight. Yet already the tawdry township below seemed to have swollen to twice the size it had been that morning.

The Scientists rode in a wide sweep that took them around this gawping crowd, and descended into the valley without recourse to the crowded path, already deeply rutted by the progress of many wheels and hooves.

"Look," Conrad called out, pointing. "The monks

71

seem to have finished.''

From their high vantage point they could easily make out the bold design the worthy brothers had forged while they had been away. The square base of the dais now enclosed an enormous wooden image of the sacred Wheel. In the centre was a representation of the sacred Hub, and, radiating from this, the wide spokes connecting the Hub with the Rim of the Wheel. That the monks had managed to produce something practical and at the same time pleasing to the eye was no mean achievement. Asquith was the first to admit it. ''They mean it to be a shrine, all right,'' he said. ''But I wonder how many the Abbot expects will worship there and pay coin into his coffers for the privilege?''

They rode across the valley to take a close look at the monks' handiwork—and found old Mallory busily haranguing the weary brothers, accusing them of interfering with *his* valley. Asquith tried to calm him down.

''But this be *my* land they make use of!'' he protested. ''It were given to me in fief, more'n twenty years past. They 'ave no right—''

''Yes, they have,'' the boy interjected, unable to resist a smile. ''They have God's right, old man.''

Asquith silenced the boy with a scowl of admonishment. He leaned down from his horse and spoke quietly to the old shepherd. ''Leave them alone, Angus. Go back to your house. Speak with the girl, Donella, and her father. They, at least will understand. But do not walk abroad too much among these people. Do you understand?''

Mallory looked at him with sick, wistful eyes, then nodded. His shoulders stooped even more than usual as he turned away from the dais and trudged back across the moist fields towards his house, muttering under his breath.

They watched him out of sight. Then Asquith urged his mount away from the monks towards the southern shore of the lake. ''Come, lad,'' he said quietly, ''let us get busy with our samples.''

The Wall burned brightly overhead. The fine network of lines had reappeared, the boy noticed, and this time they did not shift in and out of his range of vision. They seemed to have become permanently fixed. He made a mental note to mention this to Asquith.

When the Scientist thought that enough distance had been placed between the monks and themselves, he brought his mount to a stop. They both dismounted and left their horses grazing while they went about their work.

Asquith opened his leather saddlebag and withdrew one of the flasks. It had a wide neck, ideal for scooping up samples of the water. Later, he would carefully pour some of this into the small phials; these would be easier to transport.

Asquith waded out carefully into the lake. Conrad kept watch. He felt isolated. They were so far from everyone else gathered in the valley that sounds came to him blurred and indistinct; only the creaking of ox-carts could be separated from the distant hubbub. He allowed his attention to wander, just for a moment, towards the shepherd's house. He imagined that he could see Donella standing in the doorway, waving to him, but in truth it was only his imagination that conjured up her figure. Feeling suddenly angry with himself for allowing anything to interfere with his work, he turned his attention back to the lake.

By now Asquith had waded out several yards. The water lapped around the tops of his boots but he did not seem to mind, so intent was he upon his task. He stooped, staring into the water like a fisherman searching for some sign of a catch. After standing like this for what seemed a long while to the boy, he lowered the flask and scooped up some water. He made two more such passes, each time in a different direction, peering into the flask when he held it up. Satisfied, he then made his way back to the shore, a tall shadow set against the fiery brilliance of The Wall.

Back on dry land again, he pushed the cork stopper firmly into the flask with a triumphant gesture. "That will do for

73

today," he said. "Tomorrow, Conrad, we will take further samples. In this way we will be able to keep track of any increasing salinity, among other things."

The sound of rapid hoofbeats made them turn round. It was Donella. For one brief moment Conrad had a vision of her dressed in a gown, with fine, long hair streaming out behind her. He blinked: the vision was gone. Instead he saw the reality of this frail young woman dressed in a boy's clothes, yet with a heroine's disposition.

"Donella!" Asquith greeted her warmly.

She nodded, not looking at the boy. "My father sends you greetings, and asks if you might like to share our humble supper this evening—and perhaps impart to him any fresh discoveries you have made?"

Asquith gave an apologetic smile. "Convey my thanks to your father, but I regret that we cannot join him this evening. We have much urgent work to do before the morrow. By then we may have news that might interest him. If we may call at noon, perhaps?" Tactfully he avoided the real reason behind his refusal: he knew that the supply of foodstuffs in the shepherd's house barely covered their needs. He could not impose upon such generosity. Meantime, he determined to ride into Northbridge and purchase a few small supplies which he would pass on to the girl. She, at least, would understand and accept the gift, and her proud father need not know.

For a moment the girl looked crestfallen. The she pulled herself together and said, "You are both welcome to visit, any time you feel free. On no account would my father wish to interfere with your important work. Till the morrow, then."

As her mount was about to wheel away, Conrad grasped her reins. "Donella. . ."

She eyed him coldly for a moment, as though he had spoken out of turn.

"Take care," was all he could manage to say, and that

74

without looking up. "Leave the old man's house. Seek refuge at the monastery. Only ill can come of your staying in the valley. Not even your Saracen is invincble. If you had seen the likes of some we saw in Northbridge. . ."

Her face softened. "I am touched by your concern, Conrad. I will pass on your advice, but I cannot promise it will be taken. My father, as you have seen, is at odds with the Church. He is at odds with the world; that is his tragedy."

She reached out and touched him gently on the sleeve. "But thank you, just the same." For the first time something warm and trusting passed fleetingly between them. Then she was gone.

•　　•　　•

Throughout the long afternoon a festive air took command of the valley. The landscape resounded to the joyful sounds of tourney. There were impromptu jousts among the knights, and games such as the common people enjoyed. There was much drinking; canny hucksters touted their wares—wines and ales, venison and every variety of foodstuffs, for such as could afford it.

The boy and his Master watched all this from a position high on the northern rim of the valley. And as the day waned and a blazing sunset set The Wall on fire, as though the furnaces of Heaven had been stoked to their fullest, a sudden hush descended over the valley. All revelry ceased; all carnal thoughts were put aside; even minds befogged with too much drinking stood in awe of the fiery miracle stretched out across the landscape.

Even unbelievers knelt to pray. Never before, in all the chronicles of their land, had a miracle of such magnitude been made known to mankind. Yet some stood irresolute, apart from their brothers, mouths agape while they struggled to come to terms with the opposition.

"Is not nature marvellous?" Asquith whispered to the boy, his own eyes filled with wonder. Conrad could only nod; this phenomenon seemed beyond their simple capabilities to solve, yet this did not appear to worry his Master. In fact the older man did not seem in the least disturbed by the grandeur of The Wall.

"I. . . I find it a little frightening," the boy confessed, staring down into the great red cauldron below.

Asquith slapped him on the knee. "And rightly so! But that is only because we do not yet understand it." His words sounded reassuring, as though he were confident that they would succeed.

They remained at their station until dusk, when the supernal light had mostly faded from The Wall and only a trace of fiery red could be seen receding slowly to the upper edge of the phenomenon.

Their bellies rumbled, reminding them that they had not eaten for many hours. Supper would be waiting for them at the monastery; it was time for them to leave.

As they rode back through the dusk they could see many people moving out of the valley, making their way back to Northbridge. But an even greater number than before had elected to stay overnight. *Lucky for them it isn't winter,* Asquith mused. Many fires glowed in the distance, and now that the 'miracle' had faded to a pale, gossamer shimmer against the encroaching darkness, the evening gave way to a wild carouse, enough to awaken the wrath of every monk in sight.

Asquith turned to Conrad, marking his worried countenance. "You fear for the lass?"

The boy nodded.

"They would be well advised to move into the monastery. I am sure we could arrange it. . ." He was wise and generous, good Master Asquith. His words brought tears to the student's eyes.

"I did so advise. But she says her father will not go, that he holds some private war with Mother Church."

"That well may be—but if he values his daughter's safety

76

he will soon realize the wisdom of our suggestion. Keep pressing him, Conrad: he will weaken in time.''

●   ●   ●

A surprise awaited them at the monastery. A sign had been daubed in splashes of white paint on the great wooden gate. The same symbol had been liberally painted on the dilapidated hostelry outside the walls.

"What does it mean?" Conrad asked.

Asquith replied, "It is the mark of a Royal Assumption. It would seem that some nobleman and his court plan a visit here. As you know, it is their given right to take over such dwellings as they see fit. In this case it appears to be the monastery. . . and probably several of the better dwellings in Northbridge as well."

Brother Anselmo let them in. The monastery was bustling with activity, monks hurrying about this way and that in the twilight.

"I see you may expect visitors," Asquith remarked.

"Aye," the worthy brother answered. "The Duke of Bloyne and one hundred of his court." The monk threw up his hands in despair. "How we will cater for them I do not know—but my lord Abbot has told us to make preparations. Yet I cannot see how it is to be done: provide food and shelter for a hundred hungry noblemen? But who am I to question my lord Abbot?" He left them to find their own way to the stable and to their quarters, muttering to himself as he hurried away.

●   ●   ●

The Scientists shared a sparse supper. This did not unduly bother Asquith: he was eager to examine the samples of lake water they had smuggled in under his cloak, and scarcely noticed what he ate.

"The monks are much too busy to worry about us," he whispered, obviously relishing the situation. "We will be

77

able to work undisturbed tonight."

Later, in their room, the boy watched his Master light two candles on their small table. Then he carefully set down one of the glass phials and, beside it, the wide-necked flask two-thirds filled with murky water. With great care Asquith poured a quantity of this water into the small phial. This, like the flask had a flat bottom. When the phial was nearly full, Asquith set the flask aside and peered intently into the smaller vessel. From his coat he produced what appeared to be a mirror such as any rich lady might possess; it had an ornate jewelled handle and the circle of glass was surrounded by elaborately figured metal. Yet this was more than a mirror. . . .

Asquith raised the glass and looked *through* it into the phial of water. He gave a small gasp of surprise, then peered closer.

Conrad, who had been watching all the time, leaned forward. "What is it?" he asked, in a voice only slightly louder than a whisper. "Is there something in the phial?"

Very slowly Asquith shook his head. Yet this was not a negative gesture, merely one of puzzlement. Without taking his attention away from the phial he motioned to the boy to join him. "Come here, lad: take a look through the glass."

Conrad grasped the handle of the elaborate instrument, and, leaning as close as he could, peered through it into the phial of murky water.

"Tell me what you see," Asquith said quietly.

The boy concentrated. To anyone not acquainted with its properties, the glass would have seemed to possess truly magical qualities. It was one of the finest of the new magnifying lenses to have come out of Spain. Never before had the skill of these justly famous artisans so impressed the student.

The water was alive with a multitude of tiny creatures too small for the unaided eye to distinguish. But Asquith's jewelled lens magnified them by six times, presenting an

78

altogether different picture. This much had Conrad seen before; he had studied many a sample of pond water at the College, using an instrument such as this. But now. . . .

"I see. . . *something*," he exclaimed. "I see many tiny organisms. I see—" Just then something much larger flashed across his field of view. Startled, he looked up.

Asquith nodded solemnly. "That's it. Quick—" He grasped the boy by the shoulder and urged him to look again. "Follow it. Catch it. Hold it fast. Then tell me what it is you see!"

Conrad did as he was bidden. The object of his search was a creature much larger than the other tiny residents of the phial. In the lens it had looked slightly longer than an inch. But that wasn't all. . .

"I have it!" he cried, trembling with excitement.

For one brief moment the creature was held fast in the circle of his lens. It even seemed to be peering out at him, studying the boy as intently as he studied it.

Its body was fish-like, ending in a long, almost transparent tail. But it also possessed what looked like four rudimentary limbs, of equal length, and the strangest face Conrad had ever seen. It looked almost human. That is, if you could imagine a human face somehow *squashed*, with the features spread into an oval shape, the nose almost non-existent, the mouth wide and chinless, the ears flattened against the skull until they resembled nothing more than fissures, the eyes wide and protruding. The creature stayed still for quite some time, staring out at him with its strange face. Then it swam out of range. The boy was left feeling dazed, staring into the lens, but seeing nothing.

Asquith leaned over and gently took the glass from him. "Aye, Conrad," he muttered, "that is like no fish I have ever seen or heard of." He rubbed his forehead and stared into the distance. "In point of fact, I find it hard to believe this creature is of our world."

• • •

High up in the tower above his lodge, the Abbot of St Germaine no longer paced to and fro like a caged beast. Now he could even manage a smile or two when he felt like it. The vision of The Wall no longer filled him with dread or constrained him. The most marvellous idea had recently come to him. So strongly did it seem have the nature of a vision that he had convinced himself God had planted the seed of the idea in his mind.

Earlier in the evening he had made his customary visit to the abbey to pray. Peace had eluded him even there. But on leaving, he had paused for a moment by the holy reliquary by the east door. The shattered glass case had once contained a fragment, scarcely more than a splinter, of the One True Wheel, bought and brought at great expense from the Holy See itself. But he had not been blessed for long with his prize: only two years previously they had given overnight lodging to a travelling friar. The man had joined them in humble prayer in the abbey, and remarked upon their unique relic. Next morning he was gone—and so was their precious piece of the Wheel. All efforts to trace the thief came to no avail; he had worn the cassock of an unfamiliar order, a group of religious nomads, they learned later, who kept no monastery but instead roamed for ever the face of God's earth.

A monastery without a relic lacked prestige. The Abbot had been deeply mortified by their loss; he vowed that he would never again trust any traveller. And if they were ever fortunate enough to gain another relic, he would guard it with his life, day and night. So help him God.

But relics were hard to come by. And they were costly. You needed a keen eye to detect a forgery—and the good Lord knew these were numerous enough. But although the Abbot spread word throughout the land of their need they had never been presented with an opportunity to regain their prestige.

Until now. And this explained why the wily old Abbot had exchanged his trappings of woe for the gown of a smile. He could barely restrain himself from feeling smugly satisfied when he contemplated the future. Why, soon they would have more fame, wealth and prestige than any other monastery in the land—perhaps throughout Christendom, throughout the world! The loss of their tiny splinter of the Wheel seemed such a small matter when one considered the magnificence of his idea. And when the deed was done, his monastery would be blessed by the sort of boon every Abbot dreamed of in these miserable times of war and pestilence.

The more he thought about his plan, the more ecstatic the Abbot grew. He hugged himself with his scrawny arms and did a small jig around the room for joy. His eyes burned with a deep, inner fervour that matched, at times, the distant splendour of The Wall. He looked far into the future and saw the monastery of St Germaine become a shrine and place of pilgrimage for all manner of people. Thousands—nay, millions!—would journey here to behold the miracle of The Wall and receive its divine message.

A vision—and violence

That night no matins were sung. The Abbot and his worthies retired early, exhausted after their hurried preparations for the arrival of the Duke and his entourage.

Conrad woke well before dawn, drawn from his deep sleep by a dream of icy beauty. The vision clung fast to his waking mind and made his scalp tingle. *Could it be possible?*

It was bitterly cold in the room. Asquith was snoring quietly, as was his custom, with every available blanket wrapped around him. The boy drew his own bedclothes tight against him. This helped to ward off the sudden chill surrounding him, but it could not dispel the icy dream that held his mind in thrall.

He did not wish to wake his Master. Instead, he climbed quietly out of bed, pulled on his long leather buskins, and crept quietly from the room.

He found the air outside was not as still as he had supposed. There was some furtive activity afoot. Curious as to its nature, he made his way carefully through the dormitory and paused for a moment in the doorway. Clouds scudding across the moon made it difficult for him to see what was going on, but as his eyes grew more accustomed to the gloom he made out the cassocked figures of many monks scurrying busily around. They carried no lanterns, no torches, but chose to work in darkness. What were they up to? Surely this uncommon silence was not meant as a courtesy to Asquith and himself, the only guests inside the monastery grounds? The boy shook his head, puzzled. He could only assume that the monks went about their business in this fashion to ensure that they did not disturb anyone in the valley. Half a mile away? Conrad shrugged. There was obviously more to this activity than he had so far imagined.

When he concentrated he could sometimes hear furtive whispering passing to and fro between the monks, and every now and again the creak of carts and the deep rumble of labouring oxen.

The monastery gate gaped wide against a backdrop of stars. While he stood still, shivering in the bitter cold, he saw the dark outline of several carts roll out, many monks accompanying them. Then all was quiet again.

What had the Abbot ordained that had brought these men to work at such an early hour, and with such secrecy?

The boy might have pondered over this puzzle for some time, had not a more urgent matter occupied his thoughts. He hurried round to the stable, feeling the stunted grass crunch underfoot. Good: this reassured him there had indeed been a frost overnight.

He saddled his mare in darkness, fumbling only occasionally. He made sure there was no one outside before he mounted and rode quietly through the open gate.

The icy air stung his eyes and burned his cheeks, forcing him more fully awake than before. He was reminded of the many bitter cold mornings he had spent during his early days at College. . . and of a time before that which he chose to disregard.

He rode towards the northern rim of the valley. The moon was low and momentarily clear of clouds. Its rays roused The Wall into a shimmering silver half-life that looked quite eerie. Underneath, the lake seemed to glow with the same radiance in the pre-dawn landscape.

As he drew closer to the phenomenon he saw how it had been transformed while he slept, and that the vision which had intruded into his dreaming had indeed been true.

Overnight, The Wall had become a vast sheet of ice spread across the valley. The low temperature had brought down a frost that had frozen its myriad tiny water droplets.

The first faint flush of dawn had just touched the horizon when he drew level with the northern arm of The Wall. Far below he could just make out the monks and their ox-carts moving slowly down the path into the valley. A few faint creaks came to his ears, and the movement of wheels along the deep rutted path. But no other sound. Later, when the sun was fully risen, he would be able to ascertain what they were up to.

His mare picked her way carefully down the steep slope. The boy was surprised to discover that the marker he had driven into the ground now lay a good hundred yards or more downhill, so much had The Wall advanced overnight. Such a rate of growth astonished him. Why, if it maintained such a pace then it would soon outreach the valley and spread into the outside world! The prospect alarmed him; he could not imagine the consequences.

He dismounted and made his way towards the tenuous edge of The Wall. He approached it warily. At its farthest extremity, individual droplets of water had been frozen into glimmering ice-crystals. To his left, the phenomenon gradually became a solid sheet of ice stretching across the valley.

He touched this frozen crust with the fingertips of his left hand, just to confirm that his vision was real. Then he let out a sigh of relief. It had not been a dream after all: The Wall *had* frozen. The bitter cold must have reached into his mind, played around with his sleeping thoughts, and brought him this vision. How strange, how marvellous! He could hardly wait to tell Asquith.

He decided to make a bold effort. He stiffened the fingers of his left hand and plunged them *through* the icy crust.

A small portion of The Wall shattered, scattering shards on to the ground. Smaller pieces clung to his hand and began to thaw.

He laughed—a much-needed relief of tension—and began scrabbling away with both hands at the hole he had made. He pulled away several large slivers of ice and toyed with them for a moment, turning them over in his hands, marvelling at their beauty and watching his bodily warmth slowly melting them. Drops of water began to trickle through his fingers.

Gradually the eastern sky grew brighter. The moon had set while he pondered his discovery; it would not be long before the greedy sun rose and began to thaw his beautiful vision. He determined to take in every detail of the transformation, to embed it so deeply in his memory that it would remain etched there for ever.

Again he laughed; and this time there was an unmistakable edge of hysteria to the sound. A feeling of anxiety and stress suddenly overwhelmed him. Sometimes The Wall seemed to mock him with its mystery. For the first time he felt this resolve weaken; he no longer believed that Asquith or any other Scientist would ever plumb the secrets of this magnificent object. All they could do was watch and record, in as much detail as they could, its gradual transformations.

He felt frustrated that a solution to The Wall's mystery might not be granted to them. This feeling became mingled with other, deeper yearnings and soon became manifest in anger: festering hostility directed against The Wall itself.

He fumbled with his numb hands and withdrew his sword from its sheath—a sword that had never known battle or drawn human blood and had never before been drawn in anger. He raised the weapon and brought it down with all his strength against the icy face of The Wall.

It was a savage blow. The frozen crust shattered and showered him with splinters. He put so much force behind the swing that he was carried forward and *through* the great rent he had made. He stumbled and almost fell, and stood shivering on the other side of The Wall, where the frozen face of the vision could not be seen. His anger still ran riot through his system; he stamped back through the rent and stood facing the icy crust again. Then he looked down at the ground at his feet, littered with slowly melting shards of ice.

By now the sky was bright enough for him to see the whole valley quite clearly. He stepped forward and his eyes narrowed when he peered into the great gap he had slashed in The Wall. Even as he watched, tiny drops of moisture were reforming in the space his anger had created. It was as though some mysterious action was at work, sifting the water through the very pores of space.

But such things were not possible! his mind cried out. How could the air around him, the sky above, exude moisture in the way the human skin perspired? He shook his head. No. To think in that direction was madness. And yet. .

The reappearing dew began to reflect the first faint rays of the morning sun. They mocked him more gently than the great sheet of ice stretched across the valley, but mockery it was. And still his anger was not quenched. He lifted his sword again and dealt The Wall another terrible blow, this time taking care to balance himself properly. Again the ice shattered and showered all around him. Like one possessed, he struck again, again and again at The Wall, stumbling down the slope like a drunken man, hewing away at the ice and leaving behind a great rent to mark his passage. And where he had struck, new moisture slowly appeared.

Conrad cursed soundly as he flailed away at the fragile Wall. He continued hacking at it until his sword grew unbearably heavy and he had no strength left to deliver one more blow. He found himself standing near the previous day's marker, his anger exhausted.

For a while he remained there, leaning heavily on his sword, breathing erratically, his mind in turmoil. He fell to brooding upon what he had done; he could not help but compare his handiwork to that of a monstrous wound and the reappearing moisture as a soulful weeping of the sky not unlike the weeping of the flesh. And he felt ashamed for what he had done.

Ages later, it seemed, he grew aware of a touch of warmth on his shoulders. He looked around and saw that the sun had risen in all its splendour. It made The Wall blaze magnificently, as it had never done before so early in the day. But the boy knew this spectacle would last for only a wink of time; only he and the secretive monks would bear witness to it before it disappeared from view.

He watched The Wall begin to thaw, gradually losing its sudden burst of brilliance. Bitter shame still filled him; there had been no reason behind his vicious attack upon The Wall; and without reason there could never be any true science. Hadn't he been told that often enough—and didn't he believe it? *Yes.* Nonetheless, he had acted in a completely irrational manner. What would Asquith have thought of such behaviour?

Moving like someone still caught in a dream, he sheathed his sword and then looked calmly around him. There had been no one to bear witness to his disgrace; there was no need to confess it to Asquith. He would explain what had happened to The Wall overnight, but the rest he would keep to himself.

He looked around for his horse and found her waiting patiently nearby, not at all disturbed by his curious behaviour. He swung into the saddle and turned her head in the direction of the monastery. And then he paused.

Now it was bright enough in the valley for him to see clearly what the monks were about. Four ox-carts were drawn up near the wooden dais with its symbol of the sacred Wheel. And when Conrad realized just what the worthy brothers were doing, he gave a grin of pure delight.

Most had their cassocks hitched up around their thighs and were either wading into the lake to fill stout wooden casks with water, or were busy stacking the filled casks into the waiting carts. The casks were of the kind usually used for storing ale or wine, but now it seemed they were to be used to carry great quantities of water back to the monastery.

Now that he understood what they were about, Conrad was only surprised that the Abbot hadn't thought of the commercial potential of the lake earlier. No wonder the monks had begun their work at such an early hour and under cover of secrecy! Nearby, the township was still sleeping off the evening's excesses. But it would not be long before someone awoke and became curious enough to wander over and ask what was going on.

He could make out the figure of the Abbot himself in his red cassock, busily giving orders and methodically blessing each cask before it was loaded on to cart. Now that the sun was up they worked with feverish haste, not even seeming to care for the icy wonder that had existed for such a short time overhead. They were so anxious to conclude their business and get back to the monastery without arousing suspicion. He wondered how many trips they had made so far. Three? Four? He could not even guess. Surely there was a limit to the number of casks at their disposal!

He watched them for a while longer, then dug his heels into his mount and rode back to the monastery.

• • •

Asquith had been up for some time. He was in a disconsolate mood, brooding over a bowl of cold gruel. It was obvious to the boy that his Master had a great problem on his mind.

He came into the room and sat down. "We had a great frost overnight," he said, conversationally.

"Aye," Asquith agreed, without looking up. "My bones have already told me that."

Despite his Master's dour countenance, Conrad could not keep back his excitement. "Sir, this morning I have seen such a wondrous event!" And he proceeded to tell, first, of his dream and the vision it had contained, then how he had gone in search of what he had dreamed. And found it.

"It was even more beautiful than I have seen at sunset!" the boy exclaimed enthusiastically.

The older Scientist nodded, listening keenly to every word despite the thoughts that troubled him. As always, he was impressed with the detailed precision of Conrad's observation. One day he would become a great Scientist: of that Asquith felt sure.

The boy then went on to detail the activities of the monks near the lake. This seemed to interest Asquith even more than his tale of the frozen Wall—at least it brought the sparkle of amusement into his tired old eyes. But a deep frown soon chased it away. He pushed aside his unfinished gruel and leaned back heavily in his chair.

"Aye," he agreed, "I did not think it would be long before our wily old Abbot got around to thinking how he might make a penny or two out of this 'miracle'." His face grew dark and almost pained. "Conrad," he said slowly, "I am faced with a most difficult decision—and this news you have just brought me has made it even harder.—Our Wall, it seems, continues to grow at a prodigious rate. And the Abbot's activities could lead to some unpleasant disruptions in the valley. But to forget all that for a moment. . . Conrad, these samples of water we collected. That. . . creature you saw through the glass. *I must get our samples back to the college as soon as possible and have them examined with our best apparatus.*"

He gave a deep sigh and looked directly at the boy. "But who to trust with such a task, eh? Only thee and I, that goes without saying." He held up a hand to forestall the boy's impetuous offer. "Conrad, the road to Abingdon will be crawling with all kinds of thieves and vagabonds: they are drawn to a spectacle such as this as ants are drawn to spilled honey. That sword you wear with such pride, Conrad: you have never once been called upon to use it in your own defence, and I would not risk having your blood spilled. I know I can reach Abingdon, riding fast and changing horses along the way, in two days and a night. And return as quickly. But if I go—and I am convinced that I must, for time is of the essence and our samples must be studied while they are still fresh and alive—you will be left to your devices until I return. You have been well trained as an observer; you are the most reliable witness I could ask for: the report you have just given me amply supports my opinion. I am confident that I can rely on you to continue our work while I am gone, and keep a faithful record of everything that transpires. But I cannot ask something of you that I would not be prepared to do myself. Are you prepared to remain here alone, in the baleful shadow of this monastery, and keep watch on yonder Wall until I return? Think carefully now: I will not say that you lack courage if you decline.''

But Conrad's answer was prompt. He had sworn a duty to science and he was not prepared to shirk his responsibilities. Besides, his shameful action against The Wall now made him feel some sort of penance was necessary. Still, he was uneasy.

"Of course I will stay, Master Asquith. I consider the task you have set me an honourable one, and I will do my best to keep an accurate record.''

"Good lad.'' The Scientist stood up. A great weight seemed to have lifted from his shoulders. "Now, to our plans. My bags are packed and ready. But let us consider your position: in a few hours a host of courtly people will descend on this monastery. If you have never seen a Royal Assumption take place, Conrad, then you are in for a rough time, I can promise you. I shall have a discreet word with Brother Anselmo before I leave; he seems a reasonable sort of fellow, and when I have spun him a tale to explain my hasty departure, I will pass a little more coin into his palm and ask for some assurance that you will not be forgotten while I am gone. But that is all I can do. The rest will be up to you. Keep your wits about you and stay out of the wake of the Duke and his hangers-on. You will find them a cynical, world-weary lot, from all accounts. Here''—he pressed a

90

small purse into the boy's hand—"you may have need of this before I return."

Half an hour later he was gone, riding fast down the highway that led through Northbridge and on to Abingdon. He had done as he promised and spoken with the kindly Brother Anselmo; the monk stood beside the boy at the open gateway and watched his Master out of sight.

"Never thee mind, lad," he said. "We'll take care of thee. Don't worry too much about this pesky Duke and his followers. You just keep close by Brother Anselmo and you'll be taken care of." The monk smiled and patted his paunch. The palm of his hand pressed flat against the two silver coins he had secreted in his cassock. The old Abbot would not get those!

Conrad thanked the friendly monk and followed him inside. It was a while before he was able to sneak away and ride out of the monastery. He hoped Brother Anselmo would not worry too much about his whereabouts.

The boy was anxious to get down into the valley and find out what was happening around the lake. He was determined to fulfil his promise to Asquith that he would keep a careful record of every strange happening.

• • •

Quite a number of people from the township had gathered by the water's edge, watching the monks' activities in a curious silence. By now there was only one cart left standing near the wooden dais. No more appeared from the monastery. Perhaps already the Abbot felt he had overplayed his hand and had decided to call it a day.

Conrad reined his mare to a halt close by the rear of the crowd. Already the upper half of The Wall burned fiercely as it hurled back the sunlight. But the sight could not erase from his mind the magical memory of the Wall of ice.

The Abbot was standing his ground beside the dais, his crimson cloak wrapped tight around him. While the worthy brothers hefted the last of the casks on to the cart he watched the silent onlookers, his eyes narrowed as though waiting for the first signs of trouble. He was obviously prepared to defy the ugly mood that showed on some of the more unpleasant faces that stared back at him.

The pious and the profane confronted each other across an open area of hostile ground. The air seemed charged with portent. For a long while no one moved or spoke. The monks could feel a gathering anger in the crowd of onlookers and were unsure of what to do: they looked to their Abbot for direction.

Finally one of the crowd, a hulking great brute of a man with shoulders almost as broad as an ox and legs as thick as tree-trunks, stepped forward and challenged the Abbot. He scowled and his coarse words cut through the stillness like an axe.

"Mornin', Abbot," he growled, enormous hands on hips, head slightly cocked to one side. "What yer been about, eh, so early in the mornin'? An' why all these casks, eh? Not thinkin' of bottlin' the lake, are yer?" He gave a loud guffaw and threw back his head. There were a few titters in the crowd, but not much more to back him up. Most were still too unsure of their ground.

The man took a step closer.

Suddenly the Abbot thrust out his right arm to stop the giant stepping any closer. Then his thunderous voice was heard for the first time by the assembled throng, and many of them quailed and went white with fright that so much sound could emerge from such a frail-looking man.

"Listen, all of you! Let it be known far and wide that I have done this day as God willed me to do: *I have consecrated the waters of the lake.* This task He sent to me in a vision, that I might be given knowledge of the miraculous properties of the lake. He has sent His Sign in the form of this Wall in the sky; from it flows His sacred waters. They are the very tears of heaven, expressing His infinite love and patience for us." The Abbot swept out his left arm to indicate the dais. "You see where we have built a place of worship, where all are welcome. Baptisms will begin this afternoon. I will officiate at the first ceremonies. *But mark you this!*" He fixed the crowd with a cruel and penetrating stare. "This lake has been consecrated in the name of God the Father, in the manner in which He decreed. Henceforth it is the property of His Church on Earth, to be directed through our monastery of St Germaine, upon which He saw fit, in His infinite wisdom, to bestow His gift of these miraculous waters."

It was the reference to these 'miraculous' properties that proved his undoing. For some poor fools such properties took the form of an aphrodisiac, a cure-all, or eternal life. . . or you-name-it. If the Abbot had only had sense enough to keep them guessing; but his ambition overruled his reason.

The crowd's belligerent spokesman took another bold step forward. "Friend Abbot, if what you say be true, and this lake is truly miraculous, why should the Lord want the Church to keep it for the likes of themselves, eh?" He laughed loudly again, and was joined by several more louts. The crowd began to press forward.

The Abbot's face went a shade paler. He gripped his cloak until his knuckles shone white. But there was nothing he could do. The crowd was restless, in need of diversion. And one ill-chosen word on his part, that word 'miraculous', had set them off.

With what he would remember afterwards as an almost unanimous roar of triumph, the crowd suddenly surged past the dais like a herd of wild beasts and plunged fully-clothed into the lake. And there they played about and wallowed and splashed each other like happy children. The air was filled with their whooping and hollering, and this in turn drew more people to the lake.

The Abbot closed his eyes and shuddered. When he opened them he was pleased to see that not all of the crowd had acted in this unsightly manner: a handful of genuinely devout pilgrims had waded quietly into the shallows and kept well clear of the noisy rabble. They stood with their hands clasped, lips moving in prayer.

Mustering what little dignity he had in reserve, the Abbot gave the command and the last of the heavily laden carts moved off. Nobody noticed them leave. Nobody cared. Only Conrad followed them with his eyes, taking note of the sad but stately tread of the Abbot moving slowly behind the cart. He did not waste any time watching the spectacle of the crowd frolicking in the lake. Instead he rode straight towards Mallory's house, eager to impart the latest news of his discoveries to the blind knight and his daughter.

● ● ●

Donella was waiting for him in the doorway. Her face was filled with concern, and she looked a little frightened. Hakim stood at his usual position, just outside the open doorway. He nodded a curt welcome to the student, then returned his attention to the distant festivities.

Conrad explained briefly what had happened. The girl listened attentively, but the frightened expression did not leave her eyes. He wanted to reach out and comfort her, but he knew that this was neither the time or the place to do so.

"Come inside," she said. "I am sure my father will be interested at all you have to say."

He followed her inside, where, for the benefit of her ailing father, he repeated his account of what had taken place by the lake.

The knight lay on his bed. Pain showed in his face. "I heard, Donella," he said wearily. "I heard all. This young man has a voice that might raise the dead when he gets excited." He smiled, letting Conrad know the remark was not meant to slight him in any way; but this did not stop the flush of embarrassment spreading into the boy's cheeks.

The blind knight motioned him to a chair. "Sit down, lad,

I'm sure you have more to tell us."

"Aye, that I have," the boy said quickly. He pulled up the stool and sat down beside the knight. Slowly, in detail, he told them of the marvellous dream he had had, and how he had ridden out to find it come to pass in the early hours of the morning. "That was when I first knew the monks were up to something," he said.

The knight nodded, his face deep in thought. "Tell me again about the frozen Wall," he said softly. The image had obviously beguiled him. This time Conrad elaborated on his escapade, describing how he had carved great chunks of the ice out of the air. He did not tell them that this had been done in a fit of temper; he let it appear as thought it had been but more as a scientific exercise. It was a piece of not-quite-truth that Asquith would have frowned upon, but might, he thought, have condoned under the circumstances.

Donella stood behind him and to one side while he spoke. Her eyes never left him. She looked at him like one entranced, perhaps wishing she could have shared his dream and its aftermath.

"There is one other thing," the student went on. And he told them of his Master's sudden decision to return to the college in all haste. When he described the strange creature they had captured in the flask, the knight could well understand the need for such urgency.

"You say it had four limbs and the body of a fish, yet the face of a man?" he said curiously.

Conrad took a deep breath and nodded. "But a human face somehow stretched out of all proportion. I know of nothing like it—"

"Nor I!" de Vargas marvelled.

The boy looked around. His eyes met and locked with the girl's; it was heartening to see that she no longer looked upon him with defiance, but as a trusted friend. Yet he found that he could not look upon her beauty for too long. "Where is the old shepherd?" he asked innocently.

"He has taken his sheep down to the creek," she answered. "He intends to keep them out of sight of that rabble in the valley."

de Vargas stirred and leaned on one elbow. "I wouldn't worry too much about the rabble," he muttered. "The Duke's men will soon bring them to order, when they arrive."

While he agreed with the knight's observation, Conrad still remained uneasy. He had heard enough about the Duke of Bloyne and his ruthless mercenaries to suspect that they might only be trading one threat for another.

The boy stood up. "Now I must be off," he said. "I have to check the south arm of The Wall. The northern marker shows that it advanced more than a hundred yards overnight, and from what I could see from my vantage point by the lake, the waters seem to have advanced perhaps half that distance. I need to find out what has happened on the southern slopes."

The girl stepped forward. "Father, may I go with him?"

de Vargas shook his head. "No, Donella: I wish you to remain here, and keep me informed of the mood of that mob out there. Ah, don't frown so, lass—for I am sure you must be frowning!" He turned his blind face vaguely in the student's direction and said, almost apologetically, "Donella talks much of you, young man, and I doubt not that she likes you and values your friendship. But you must understand that I do not wish her to go too far abroad."

The boy said, "I understand."

"I know you are alone now," de Vargas went on. He paused, frowned, then went on: "I would send Hakim with you, but I fear our need of him is the greater."

"That is quite true," the boy said. "Do not bother yourself about my safety. I have learned from a Master." And with that he took his leave, thanking de Vargas for his hospitality and endevouring to charm Donella with a smile. But her expression remained strangely distant. He could not

96

understand why. He hurried outside. Women—even young girls—could be inscrutable at the very best of times. He determined not to let it bother him for the moment; he had much important work to do.

● ● ●

When finally he reached the tenuous southern edge of The Wall, he discovered that it had advanced in proportion to its northern arm: his marker lay a good hundred yards downhill. Far below he could see the people still disporting themselves in the lake, turning it into a muddied trough.

The Abbot got the best of the bargain, he mused wryly. At least his casks would contain relatively pure and unsullied water, not the murky stuff he saw below. Far to his right and behind the shepherd's house, he could see Mallory leading his flock down a steep declivity that ran alongside the bed of the tiny creek. *Poor Mallory. . .*

He drove another marker into the ground to indicate the present extent of The Wall, cursing himself for not having done the same around the other side before he came this far. But there was still time.

He rode slowly around the western rim of the valley, pausing to study the landscape from the other side of The Wall. The strange distortions persisted. In fact, they seemed to be even more pronounced than on the previous day. Tents and stalls were squat and ugly; little people scuttled around on skimpy legs with swollen bodies and flattened heads. For a moment Conrad was reminded of the curious face in the phial; the memory brought with it a shudder.

He made a mark in his book of records that the outward curvature of The Wall seemed to have increased by a few degrees; like the distortion-effect, it was certainly more pronounced than before. The effect was disturbing.

He noted with some concern that from this side of The Wall, the monks' wooden dais looked more like a rectangle than a square, and that it was only a few hundred yards from the lake shore. If the latter continued to expand at its present rate, in another few days the dais would be under water! Of course the Abbot could not have realized this; his was not a scientific mind. *Should I tell him?* Conrad wondered, briefly. But such advice would surely expose his mission, and that could lead to only one conclusion. . . Another shudder, this one more deeply felt than before. *Leave them to it, then.*

It was almost midday and Conrad had not eaten for some time. Yet he did not feel hungry. Excitement and mystery had closed his stomach into a tight knot. He thought of Asquith, and wondered if his Master would indeed make the journey to Abingdon and back as swiftly and safely as he had hoped. Then his thoughts turned to the enigmatic Donella and her father. And Hakim. To think that the Saracen had seemed so fearsome at first! Almost he had begun to feel a part of their close-knit family. He had been alone in the world for all but two of his sixteen years, and this solitude had weighed heavily upon him. Yet he had dedicated his life to the service of Science, just as, years before, when he had been but a child, he had dedicated his youthful aspirations to another order. . .

Eventually his train of thought led him back to the strange creature he had seen in Asquith's phial. Mostly he remember the oddly human way it had peered back at him through the magnifying-glass, as though it were studying him with an identical exercise of its alien mentality.

After a while he resumed his ride. He took his time, going around the western rim of the valley and looking every now and again through the strange distorting lens of The Wall at the goings-on in the valley.

He descended to the northern edge of The Wall and placed a marker. Then he stood back to survey the sudden turn of events taking place below.

The festive air had been disrupted by too many high spirits. There were sudden outbreaks of violence, as though these people had brought with them restraints they had harboured for many bitter years. Fights began to break out. Before long the shore of the lake became an arena for the crawling crowd. When the boy looked closely he saw that the brilliant light cast by The Wall showed the turbulent water stained with blood. He saw several bodies floating face-down, with no sign of life.

Oh, my God! he thought. *What is happening?* Had everyone down there gone mad? Was there no sensible leader among them to bring them to their senses?

His alarm increased. He thought immediately of Donella, and of her helpless father.

He remembered Asquith's admonishment to remain inside the monastery, under Brother Anselmo's wing. But surely his Master could not have foreseen this sudden outbreak of violence. The boy found his loyalty suddenly torn in two, but only for a moment was there doubt in his mind. Then the matter was settled. For the time being his place was with Donella, her father, Hakim and the old shepherd—at least until this violence wore itself out.

He remounted and rode back up the steep slope. He did not descend immediately into the valley, but rode back the way he had come, around the western rim. It was longer, but safer. All the while he kept a keen eye on the events taking place below.

And he was the first person to witness from afar the arrival of the Duke of Bloyne and his long cavalcade of men and coaches.

The valley of the shadow

It was mid-afternoon when the entourage drew to a halt out-side the gates of the monastery. The Duke's private coach was supported slightly askew on four ill-sprung wheels and wore a sad patina of flaking purple paint. It was drawn by four jaded horses.

The coach was preceded by a company of forty footsore archers, and before them rode a dozen knights or more, wearing dilapidated chainmail, their spirits low. Theirs had been a long and difficult journey. At last they had arrived. Only a few of them looked back to where the royal coach stood by the open gate of the monastery; most stared ahead at the remarkable apparition hanging over the valley.

Behind the Duke's coach rode six of his officers, a dour group of men with drawn faces and irritable expressions. And after them a long line of carriages and weary foot soldiers seemed to extend almost to the horizon. In all there might have been a hundred and forty souls gathered together under the Duke's banner. The tailend of the cavalcade pre-sented a dismal array of court hangers-on, their clothes and conveyances tattered and almost worn-out, like their owners. Each one of them had seen better times, and for this reason alone the doddering old Duke would go nowhere without them. They were living relics of a nobler time. They were his contemporaries; many had fought at his side before the Partition.

A few moments after his coach had rolled to a stop, the Duke poked his head out of the window to see what had

100

caused the delay. They had been travelling for so long, it had not occurred to him they might have arrived at their destination.

When his watery eyes fastened upon The Wall and its blazing surface of sunlight, his mouth froze open in an 'O' of astonishment. Nor was he alone in this reaction. All along the cavalcade of newcomers, men and women stood gaping in amazement at the phenomenon they had heard so much about, and travelled so far to see. Even hard-headed soldiers and faithless knights felt something move deep inside them, and many squirmed from the discomfort.

A tall, grim-faced figure wrapped in a scarlet cloak strode out from the monastery to greet the new arrivals.

"My lord Duke," the Abbot called out, his voice carrying an authoritative yet respectful ring. "You have come at last!"

"Eh?" The Duke slid across to the other side of his coach and peered out of the window on that side. He stared at the Abbot, measuring the man with a glance while at the same time struggling to recall what he had seen through the other window. "Well, of course I've arrived! Isn't that obvious? You must be the Abbot. . . of St Germaine."

The Abbot bowed low. "That is correct, my lord Duke. I bid you welcome in the name of God's church. Your quarters are prepared. We have done what we could to make space and provide for your. . . court. I hope, my lord, you will find it pleasing."

"Yes, yes. Quite, quite." The Duke fluttered a limp hand, indicating his boredom with protocol. He was tired and thirsty and anxious to take a bath. Then he would have a closer look at the miracle he had glimpsed from his carriage.

The Abbot took a deep breath and stepped forward. "My good Duke," he said, sounding a note of urgency, "before you alight I would implore you to command your soldiers to restore order in the valley! There are several hundred pilgrims down there already; fights have broken out, the holy

101

lake has been despoiled; disorder is rampant. They are making a mockery of the very God they have come here to worship. I fear for the safety of innocent lives. . . for us all, unless something is done quickly. If you would but order your soldiers—''

The Duke frowned. Until now his deafness had not enabled him to hear the din rising from the valley, but when he concentrated he could hear the far-off noise of a rabble in full cry. "The devil you say," he muttered. Then, realizing the unfortunate slip of the tongue, he cleared his throat. "These waters are sacred?" he asked.

The Abbot nodded vigorously. "I consecrated the lake myself, only this morning. God came to me in a vision and told me this should be done, so that the miraculous properties of the water could be preserved. . ." He went on to describe briefly the miracle of The Wall and the despicable conduct of so many who were supposed to have come to worship. (Later, the Abbot told himself, there would be more business to discuss with the Duke: he had devised a plan whereby they would both be made wealthy, and the sanctity and the safety of the valley assured.) But for the moment he was only concerned with suppressing the outbreak of violence among the 'pilgrims'.

The Duke heard him out. He sighed. "Oh, all right then. If it's as bad as you say. . ."

"Probably much worse now, my lord."

"Aye. My men will attend to it. Officers!" he bawled, and immediately fell into a fit of coughing. Highway dust had made a ruin of his lungs for these many days.

The Abbot bowed. "Thank you, my lord." And backed away as the officers rode up and took up their position beside the Duke's coach. They conferred briefly, nodding their heads. Then two rode to the head of the column and made a quick consultation with the group of archers. Another two galloped to the rear of the coach to confer with the cavalry.

The Abbot crept back inside the monastery. With a creaking noise the Duke's coach started up again and surged forward; obviously he intended to have a closer look at the valley before returning. The remainder of his entourage remained patiently in ranks; only the cavalry and a detachment of foot soldiers filed grimly past the open gate.

Conrad saw the Duke's coach appear at the entrance to the valley and the crowd there quickly disperse as soldiers pushed them aside.

There was a short delay before the archers began to advance casually down the steep path. Those still brawling in the valley seemed unaware of what was about to descend upon them; those who were not fighting were too busy watching their fellows to pay any heed. But the boy knew what was about to happen.

His scalp prickled with a growing sense of danger. . . and urgency. He dug his heels into his mount and moved into a gallop. It was imperative that he reach the old shepherd's house before. . . he hesitated to think any further. A moment later he was over the rim of the valley and almost sliding down the steep slope, praying that his mount would not lose her footing.

Meanwhile the archers marched down the well-worn path with the mindless purpose of mill-wheels. So preoccupied was the brawling, hysterical mob that they failed to notice this vanguard of the Duke's soldiers until they were almost upon them. Behind the archers, at a discreet distance, rode a number of hand-picked cavalrymen, and beside them, a complement of footsoldiers.

Conrad reached the floor of the valley in record time. He did not waste a moment but angled towards the house, casting a quick glance in the direction of the lake and the advancing soldiers. Overhead the towering glory of The Wall had been forgotten by the crowd. The air was filled with animal cries and, farther away, the sounds of weeping women. For a moment all this seemed to freeze into a frightening tableau that burned deeply into the boy's mind, reminding him of a canto of Gower's epic poem, *Gates of Hell*. . .

The archers came to a halt. They formed ranks and raised their crossbows. At a word from their leader they fired without warning into the crowd. The heavy shafts bit deep into human flesh; everywhere people fell screaming in agony, some wounded, some dead.

The archers regrouped and rewound their bows. But a second volley was not forthcoming. Instead, the ragged column of cavalry swept past them, straight into the now terrified crowd. Lances were lowered and jabbed indiscriminately around. Horses shouldered people aside, sending them sprawling into the mud. There were screams as others struggled to get out of the way of the ferocious charge. Some were successful; some were knocked over and trodden down or sent to their death by the brutal lance thrusts. A handful were mindful enough to dive into the lake and swim for their lives out of reach of the horses; for a while they trod water and watched the carnage in comparative safety. Above them The Wall glared down dispassionately, like a backdrop to some tragic play.

Conrad reached the house at full gallop. He leapt from his horse, tethered it to the barn, and rushed around to the door.

Donella was standing alone in the doorway, one hand raised to her cheek while she looked out in horror at the terrifying spectacle.

"Donella!" he cried, making her start with surprise.

"Inside—quickly! Don't let anyone see us! There is no telling what those men are capable of. . ."

He bustled her inside, past the towering figure of the Saracen, into the centre of the room. Hakim gave him a warm nod.

"Conrad?" de Vargas was sitting on the edge of his bed. "Thank God you have come! We had such fear for your safety, lad."

"And I for yours! Ah, such madness has been unleashed out there such as I have never seen."

The blind knight nodded. "We will be safe here. The Duke is only doing what needs to be done. That rabble must to be subdued, and his troops are the men to do it. Awful, bloody work, lad, but not as bad as you would have seen if you had accompanied me to the Wars."

Feeling somewhat dazed, the boy sank down upon the stool. He rubbed his forehead, then looked up at Donella. "I think it would be wise to close the door," he said. "You can watch. . . through the window."

She nodded, and inclined her head to Hakim. The Saracen stepped forward and closed and locked the stout wooden door. The he walked over to the open window and maintained his vigil.

"You look pale. . . and hungry," Donella said gently. "I will get you something to eat and drink."

"Thank you," he stammered. It had not occurred to Conrad that his feeling of dizziness was partly caused by the fact that he had hardly eaten anything during the day. He thanked the girl when she put a plate before him; it contained bread and a piece of dry sausage, and she gave him a mug of red wine. He ate slowly and sipped carefully at the wine.

Gradually the sounds of terror faded. Donella joined the Saracen by the window.

"What are they doing now?" Conrad asked, without turning around.

"They appear to be driving the people back to their tents and dwellings," she said. If she felt any anguish for the people in the valley, it was not evident in her voice. She reported events as if she were far removed from them. In such a way had life. . . trained her. Never to come too close to feeling.

"Aye," de Vargas mumbled, lolling back on his bed. "They'll soon have them orderly again. Then I wonder what our canny old Abbot will do, eh?"

Later they heard a trumpet blow shrilly, three times, recalling the Duke's men. The archers withdrew several hundred yards then stood lounging around, awaiting further orders. The cavalry routed the last of the mob from the lake and sent them scurrying back to their township. Only the dead and wounded were left to occupy the stretch of land between the lake and the settlement.

For the remainder of the afternoon Donella reported faithfully to her father everything that transpired in the valley. She never once spoke to the boy and did not seem inclined to even warm him with a look. But so much had happened, of such dreadful import, that her coldness did not affect him. Conrad's mind was in turmoil. He had no idea of what he should do next. *Oh, Asquith—why are you not here? You would know what to do !*

Time passed. Another trumpet sounded. A company of footsoldiers spread out and formed a cordon between the lake and the township. An uneasy silence settled over the land, broken only by the feeble cries of the wounded and the dying who still lay unattended. The lake was swollen with a heavy burden of bodies floating face-down, and discoloured by the oozing darkness they spread about.

The fiery sunset was admired by the Duke and his men but for the most part went unnoticed by the grim-faced people huddling together in the valley. A few lanterns had been lit in the township; a brooding anger and desire for revenge against the Duke lapped at every man's heart.

Now that order had been established, the Duke and his officers returned to their lodgings at the monastery, where the Abbot waited with avarice in his heart.

At dusk, soldiers could be seen moving around in the shallow water by the lake's edge, hauling the dead bodies out of the water and piling them on the shore. Others roved around among the dead and wounded, despatching from this world with a quick thrust of the knife any who seemed near the edge of death. A rousing kick was delivered to anyone found faking, and much laughter was aroused at the sight of these hapless folk scurrying back to the township. Those who were unable to walk were helped back by a few of their more courageous fellows. And all the while the Duke's men performed their macabre duties with the bored indifference of professional soldiers.

Conrad and Donella stood watch together by the open window, staring out into the gathering darkness. He felt at ease now that the initial action was over and they had escaped the massacre.

The girl lifted her head and looked up at the fiery strip of crimson that marked the upper edge of the marvellous Wall. "I do not think it would be wise for you to attempt to reach the monastery tonight," she said softly. "I have discussed the matter with father, and he is of the same opinion. You may stay with us, if you wish." She did not move her attention away from the sky.

Conrad was taken aback. He had not given any thought to what conditions would be like at the monastery, or how the Duke's soldiers would take to a lone horsemen setting out across what had only a few hours earlier been a battlefield. "Why. . . that is very generous of you," he said lamely. "But I have no bed, no blankets. And you have only enough for yourselves."

She turned and flashed him a smile. "It has already been arranged. You will sleep in the barn. There is clean straw there, and I have discovered an old blanket or two tucked away. Provided you do not mind the company of our horses, I think that promises to be a safer lodging than yonder monastery."

There could be no denying the wisdom of her words. He was much touched by her thoughtfulness. "Thank you, Donella. Perhaps in the morning I will be able to make my way back to the monastery without being challenged."

"In the meantime you need a place to rest. Wait a moment—I'll get you a candle."

107

He heard a trumpet sound again: four long notes, announcing a curfew none dared challenge. Bonfires were lit along the cordon of foot soldiers and the boy could hear jokes being bandied back and forth between the men. A selected company of the Duke's cavalry patrolled the lake.

"Here, Conrad. . ."

He felt her weight against him. He must have looked worn-out, for the girl was moved to take his arm and rest her cheek against his shoulder. "Come, now. You must have sleep if you are to carry out your work tomorrow."

Work? How would he be able to carry out his important tasks with these troops around? *Oh, Asquith—hasten!*

"Come. . ." She tugged at his arm. He felt a sharp pang when the gentle weight of her cheek was lifted from his shoulder. He nodded, rubbed his weary eyes and did as he was bidden.

"Hakim," she whispered, "open the door for our young friend."

High overhead the last touch of colour had faded from The Wall. Except for the jocular remarks of the soldiers, the air was still. And the tattered remnants of the day crept away with bloodied hands.

●　　●　　●

Alone in his eyrie, The Abbot was dancing a wild jig for joy. He had consumed more than his usual share of the evening's ale and this, combined with his successful negotiations with the Duke, had left him deliriously lightheaded.

The Duke had agreed that his men should police the valley to maintain order. In return, he would receive one-half of all proceeds from the sale of the 'sacred' water, while the Abbot would also receive one-half of the toll fee which the Duke intended to extract from everyone who came to the valley.

That so much worldly power had suddenly fallen into the Abbot's lap—well, not strictly *fallen;* he had engineered most of it by stealth and cunning—overwhelmed him slightly. But he had no doubt that in time he would grow accustomed to his new position. In time he would become one of the most powerful influences in the land; his alliance with the Duke would ensure this.

What were a few simple lives, more or less? And in particular the sort of lives the troops had despatched with such nonchalant ease? The Lord Himself plucked them like weeds from the earth, whether by war or by plague. So, in the long run, what did it matter?

The grim spectre of power and prestige had arrived to dominate the winter of the Abbot's life. He was even prepared to challenge God Himself on the right of his enterprise. He danced and danced until he fell into a swoon. Then slept more soundly than he had since the coming of The Wall.

Nine

Many dimensions

Donella spent a sleepless night, haunted by dark memories dredged from the past by the outbreak of violence in the valley. She saw again through the frightened eyes of a ten-year old child the sacking of her father's castle, the brutal murder of her mother. . . and other events she would have wished removed from her mind altogether, if that were possible. But it was not: the memories would be with her for ever.

She rose early and made some herb tea. Mallory and her father slept soundly: the latter's deep, apparently dreamless sleep surprised her. She had expected him to have a troubled night, like herself, with many a hideous memory of battle resurrected by the sound of so much killing. But this did not seem to have bothered him as much as she had expected. The random brutality of the Duke's soldiers had shocked her far beyond anything she had seen since the loss of their ancestral home. But she reminded herself that her father was, after all, a soldier, and had seen worse in his time.

The old shepherd and his faithful hound were curled up in their customary position by the fireplace, huddled together for mutual warmth, Mallory had watched the actions of the Duke's soldiers from afar, and deemed it unwise to return to his own house lest he be caught up in the carnage. So he had bided his time and crept back stealthily under cover of nightfall.

Donella moved around listlessly: thoughts other than those of violence were troubling here, and were not so easily put aside. She coaxed a fresh glow from the few smouldering embers by scattering a few handfuls of dry grass over them, and when these caught she added some twigs, then larger pieces of wood until she had a small fire burning. She boiled water in an old iron pan and added to it some herbs she had picked and ground the day before. Gradually a pleasant aroma began to fill the room; it brought a faint smile to her weary face and an anticipation of warmth to her body.

Both men were still sleeping soundly. She saw no point in waking them. Let them slumber on; they would need all the rest they could get to refurbish their strength.

When the tea had brewed long enough she poured some into a mug and took it out to Hakim. The Saracen was at his usual post, squatting just outside the door, his head bent forward and resting upon his knees. But he looked up quickly when he heard the sound of the door opening. Donella motioned him to stay where he was and handed him the steaming mug of tea.

She looked out across the valley. It was just first-light, yet already there was much activity. Some carts and tumbrils had been commandeered by the Duke's men, and even now the last of the dead were being carried away. In all, perhaps fifty people had been slain the previous day; the thought made her shudder. If she and her father had happened to have been among that motley crowd—even on the outskirts, together with some of the more genuine pilgrims, then they too might have made their exit from the world.

Hakim sipped his tea, brooding over what he saw. He must have sensed what the girl was thinking, for he gave her a look she knew well: his face creased into an almost apologetic grimace. It was his way of letting her know that they were in the presence of evil deeds. The Saracen's communications were rare, but there was never any lack of rapport between them at a time of crisis. She felt very close to her protector at this moment. She touched him lightly on the shoulder, then went back inside.

She poured two more mugs of tea and went out again. She

nodded with her head in the direction of the barn, indicating to the Saracan that she was taking some of the tea to the young student. Hakim eyed the two mugs, nodded enigmatically, and returned his attention to the valley.

●　　●　　●

The barn had been cobbled together out of old timbers years ago. It had never been meant to hold more than a few head of sheep and perhaps some pigs, along with such winter fodder as the old shepherd could stockpile: now it was filled to capacity.

Donella's first impression, as she pushed her way through the rickety wooden doors, was of the overpowering odour of horseflesh and its accompanying smells. If it were not for the abundant ventilation provided by the gaping chinks and holes in the walls, it would have been quite impossible for anyone to have shared such a confined space with horses.

Conrad was awake when she entered. He, too, had found it nearly impossible to sleep; what with the incredible events of the previous day crowding his head, and the proximity of so much horseflesh.

He was in the far corner of the barn, sitting up on his makeshift bed of straw. The knight's cart had been rammed up against the back wall beside him. Their three horses had been hitched to this, and had just enough room between them to remain reasonably calm. Conrad's mount was hitched to the wall on the opposite side of the barn, almost at his feet, where his saddle now rested.

His face was haggard in the early morning light. She managed a welcoming smile and went straight to him, kneeling down beside him. She held out one of the mugs. "Herb tea," she said. "Freshly made."

She could see that he was only half-awake, his mind still befogged from lack of sleep. He hardly looked like a boy at all, and she wondered as to what had caused this subtle transformation: surely there was something more going on in

112

his mind than the events they had witnessed yesterday?

Conrad mumbled his thanks and held the mug with both hands for a moment so that he could feel the warmth seeping into his fingers and the sweet-smelling aroma penetrating his head.

"You are. . . most kind," he said.

The horses snorted and stirred restlessly, as though they resented the girl's intrusion. She hushed them to be quiet. Then she shifted her body so that she was sitting beside Conrad, her legs spread out; she rested her weight on her left elbow.

"The soldiers have taken the dead away," she told him. "They must have got some carts from the monastery—or taken them from the people in the valley. Either way, they're gone."

Conrad frowned. "They are abroad then, so early?"

She nodded. "I would imagine they are keen to clean the place up for whatever it is the Abbot proposes to do."

The boy coughed. The tea was so hot and strong it had made his nose run. He fumbled in the pocket of his jerkin for a kerchief, feeling foolish.

"Here," said the girl. "Use mine."

"Thank you." He mopped his face in embarrassment. "It's. . . the tea."

She laughed softly. "I know," she said. "But that's the only way to take it: hot."

He was amazed at her friendliness. Now, she seemed a different person to the ragamuffin he had first met, who had challenged his 'book learning'. She seemed relaxed, as if she was glad to have found a friend amid so much tragedy. For his part, he was much pleased this was the direction their relationship had taken.

"How is your father?" he asked. By now the pungent tea had begun to take effect and had roused his torpid mind.

"He slept well enough. I had expected otherwise, what with the events of yesterday. I am thankful, Conrad, for I could count on the fingers of one hand the nights he has slept peacefully this past year.''

She sipped slowly at her tea, in an elegant manner completely at odds with her ragged, boyish attire. Her face had softened; she smiled at him over the edge of her mug. "You did not sleep so well," she added.

"Nor you," he countered. The deep lines around her dark eyes showed as much.

She said: "There is a creek behind the house. The water will be quite cold, but a quick bathe might help put some life back into you. If you like I'll keep watch for you while—"

When she saw the outraged look on his face she realized her mistake, and was unable to do anything but cover the bottom of her face with one hand and give a girlish giggle to conceal her own embarrassment. Eventually she managed to control her mirth. "I'm sorry, Conrad. Forgive me. Sometimes even *I* think of myself as a boy!"

The deep flush faded slowly from Conrad's face. He forced himself to consider her strange way of life, thrust upon her out of grim necessity. "It must be. . . very hard for you," he said gently.

"No more so than it is for many poor folk. At least we have Hakim."

Aye, he thought. *And a blind father. . .*

He leaned forward. "Tell me a little about your father, Donella. This blindness—how did he come by it?"

She shook her head sadly. "That I know not. He will not speak of it—although there have been times, when he has been pressed about his experiences, or in his cups, when he has returned time and again to the terrible siege of Krakow. If he lost his sight anywhere, then I think it must have been there. But he will not say, and it is not wise to press him too far, for he can fly into a most dreadful rage."

"Yes, I can understand that. I hear that the heathen Slavs have mastered the art of hurling fire at their enemies. The nature of the burns on your father's face seem to indicate such a wound. And yet. . ." He paused, not quite sure if he should continue. But Donella was listening attentively, with no sign that he was saying anything amiss. So he went on.

"I cannot say for certain," he said, "but I believe that there is a possibility your father's blindness and those terrible scars were not caused by the same incident. Donella, have you never known men—and women, too, for that matter—struck dumb for a time by something so terrible they have seen that they cannot bear to speak of it? I have known this condition to last for weeks—months—years. I have been told it can even last a lifetime. *Have* you had any contact with what I have described?"

The girl nodded reluctantly.

"Well then, what I am suggesting is simply this: we know your father is not yet completely blind, that he can distinguish between light and dark. I would not wish to plant any false hopes in your mind, but it does seem possible that he may have been *struck blind* in a similiar manner by the terrible things he has been through. Why should the eyes be so different from the tongue? Think upon what I have said."

She gave him a strange look. "Are you saying that my father may one day see again?"

The boy nodded. "It is—possible. But only when he wills it to be so. Of course I may be wrong. But I should like Master Asquith to examine your father: he is more learned than I in such matters. Do you think he would consent to a few simple tests? Mark you, I am not saying we or anyone else can cure him of his blindness: but if my theory be correct, then mayhap we can encourage a cure within himself. Say nothing of this to your father: I would not wish to disturb him in any way whatsoever. But if you will bear in mind what I have said, and cease to regard his blindness as irreparable, then perhaps something yet may be done to save his sight. All I am asking is that you do not cease to hope."

There was a long silence. The girl sipped moodily at her

tea, finally placed it aside. She sat quite straight, her arms wrapped around her knees, and stared at him. "Your theories about my father's blindness make interesting talk, master Conrad." There was a faintly mocking edge to her words. "Pray tell me, have you worked out a theory that might explain yonder Wall?"

If she had expected to catch him off-guard, she was disappointed. A look of triumph suddenly appeared on the boy's face. "Yes . . . yes, I believe I have, Donella! Just a beginning, mind you. But if I work on it long enough. . ."

He told her then that he had been up at dawn, even before she had began making her tea. He had stepped outside the barn and studied The Wall in the early-morning light, oblivious to the comings and goings of the Duke's men. He told her how he gauged the lake to have advanced a good hundred yards overnight: only a short distance now separated the water from the Abbot's wooden dais.

"We may soon have to vacate the shepherd's house," he said. "By tomorrow morning it may be awash."

Then where would they go?

"But how can you know this?" the girl asked, suddenly frightened. "How can you say that such a thing will be so?"

The boy sighed. "I cannot say for sure, Donella: I can only surmise there is a high probability that this will indeed occur."

He went on to explain how The Wall had acquired a curiously mottled appearance and had become even more convex, projecting forward over the lake by many degrees.

"It continues to expand, and so does the lake. There is no indication that this expansion will cease."

Donella gazed at him in fascination. It was hard for her to visualize what he was saying; her mind had not been trained to understand such things. Conrad seemed to realize this, for he lowered his voice and said gently, "Donella, I know how difficult this must be for you: but try to understand. It is my task—my sworn duty—to observe anything strange, to

116

record what I have seen; and, where possible, to make conjecture upon what I have seen. This much I have done."

She eyed him coldly. "You said you had a theory."

Her attitude exasperated him. He put down his empty mug and got up from his bed of straw. "Wait a moment," he said, and walked over to where he had pitched his saddle on the floor. He rummaged around in one of its pouches for a moment, then withdrew a small, leather-bound book. He walked back with a smile of triumph and sat down cross-legged on his bed, facing the girl.

"This is my personal notebook," he explained. "Not my Book of Records. This is . . . a kind of log. A log of things which I have read that have interested me greatly and have played a great part in shaping my life. But I warn you: if it should fall into the hands of someone like, say, our wily old Abbot, then I might easily be imprisioned—or worse."

The girl looked puzzled. "But *why,* Conrad?"

"Why?" He smiled grimly as he leafed slowly through the small pages of the book, scanning them briefly here and there. "Because I have reproduced certain passages from volumes forbidden by the Church." His voice dropped to a whisper as he confided in her. "In our College we have a few remaining copies of some of these valuable books. The rest were burned by order of the Inquisition."

"But if they are so valuable, why did the Church destroy them?"

"Because they dared to ask questions which the Church would rather have suppressed."

She regarded him blankly. She could not understand how a mere book could threaten anything as firmly established as the Church.

"Listen," he went on, in hushed tones. "I will explain to you how a book can become so powerful." He tapped his notebook. "Here, for example, I have written down in my own hand passages from one of the greatest works ever conceived by the human mind, which the Inquisition condemned

117

as blasphemy. . ."

And he told her a little about this work, *A Dialogue On The Nature of Dimensions, Including Space and Time,* and a little about the man who had written it. He was called Galileo.

"For most of his life," Conrad explained, "this marvellous man was fascinated by the nature of our world, and the way in which we perceive it. He was not of our Guild; it was long before our time. But he was one of the first of the truly great Scientists. It is mainly because of this man that we possess the spirit of inquiry that is the basis of our work.

"Late in his life Galileo came to the conclusion that, if there were an infinite number of possibilities that could arise from any given action, then it was quite likely that an infinite number of dimensions, of worlds other than our own, existed. The reason that we can never see them, he argued, is because they exist independently and are separated from our world by the complex nature of space and time as we imagine it. You see, he could not believe that life as we know it was simply a procession of nights and days leading ultimately to the grave. In his famous work, Galileo even suggests that there could be other dimensions where worlds very like our own exist, but are subtly different.—For example, a world where you and I never met; where there were never any Crusades against a crazed Slavonic prophet; where Columbus did not find a land route to the orient. And so on. *Perhaps even a world where the Holy Christian Church does not exist.*

"*Now* do you understand why he was called before the Holy See and sent for trial before the Inquisition? Although Galileo never went so far as to state in print what I have just said, such was the interpretation placed upon his book by the Church. And that was blasphemy.

"What did he do, this tired old man, who knew very well what the instruments of torture could do to his frail old

118

body? He was made to recant, to publicly declare that there were 'only three dimensions: height, length, and depth'. Then he was spared to spend the rest of his life in exile, watched over by the Church.'' Conrad paused.—"There is, however, a tale that, as he was being led from the place of Inquisition, he was heard to mutter irritably, 'There are *still* more than three! I like to think that story is true—it would be so like the true nature of the old fellow!''

The girl was overwhelmed by all Comrad had told her. She had great difficulty following his words. Much of what he said was beyond her. One thing above all had impressed: the possibility of worlds other than their own. "Other worlds . . ." she murmured.

"All Galileo's work might have remained mere theorizing,'' Conrad went on, warming to his topic, "had he not made allowance for one crucial point. He postulated that, given an infinite number of worlds separate from our own, it was possible that, from time to time, weakness might become apparent in the fabric of space and time that kept *our* world separate. And *vice versa,* over and over again. And where these weaknesses occurred it was possible that there might be an interchange between one world, one dimension, and another. Seeking to establish this Theory, he turned to the crowded mythology of our past. To creatures such as dragons, gryphons and chimerae, the likes of which we have never seen again. And strange disappearances. . . and re-appearances. Alas, it was only in his last remaining years that he began to explore these reports and link them to his theories. We have a Master Fort at our College who has taken it upon himself to make as thorough an Investigation as possible into all past sightings of this nature, and so complete as best he can the marvellous work begun by the great Galileo.''

Donella's head was reeling. It was all too much for her mind to absorb. For a moment she felt quite faint. She raised a hand to her face and looked as though she might swoon.

"Donella!'' The boy leaned forward and grasped her

119

gently by the shoulders. "Forgive me. I. . . I sometimes get carried away when I speak of Galileo. He was such a great man. . . and he suffered greatly at the hands of the Church."

She pulled herself together. "I am all right," she said. "It is just. . . so much."

He smiled at her and said gently: "Then think for a moment upon this little thing: how do you imagine our world might look, viewed, say, through the eyes of a frog, or an ant, or a bird? Again, think upon your shadow before you, when you stand in the sunlight. It is but a *two* dimensional representation of your three dimensional body! Is it not possible that our three-dimensional world may be but a representation of a *four*-dimensional world we are incapable of perceiving? These and many other questions become part of the great theory Galileo envisaged. It is our task, as Scientists, to continue the work that he and others began so long ago."

Donella looked at him with a bewildered and vulnerable expression. He no longer sounded like a book when he spoke; his words were alive with enthusiasm, with passion. He *believed* so much in what he. . . preached.

"Oh, Conrad," she said. "I feel so wretched." And she shivered.

"Are you cold, Donella?" He made to take off his jerkin and put it around her shoulders.

"No. Only. . . frightened."

"Of me? Of anything I have said?"

She hesitated. "No, not really." It was apparent that she did not wish to discuss the reasons for her disquiet, and he did not press her. "Tell me," she said. "how do your great Galileo's theories explain The Wall?"

The boy frowned. "That I am still pondering. But it does seem likely that, if there are other dimensions, other worlds, such as he predicted, and if weaknesses do occur from time to time at certain points which he called 'interfaces', then our

Wall may be just that: a sudden coming together of two different worlds, a weakness that has occurred in this local area of space and time. Beyond that I have no idea. There is much work that yet needs to be done—"

"And which the Duke and his soldiers will probably ensure you are not allowed to pursue," she broke in.

Conrad sighed. "That I fear."

"Have you finished your tea?"

"Yes, thank you. I. . . I hope I haven't bored you with all my talk?"

She smiled. Her nervousness seemed to have left her.

"On the contrary, you have stirred my wits no end, Conrad, with all your wild talk of. . . of other worlds."

His face grew stern. "Do you remember something your father said, how this world of ours seems such an ill-matched patchwork? Well, I have often thought much the same myself. Donella, this is the seventeenth century: *one thousand six hundred and eighty-three years since the birth of the Child.* Has it never occurred to you that surely by now our world should have amounted to more than scattered groups of small and constantly warring communities? Has it never bothered you that the Church, which could have become such a bastion of real knowledge, is instead a tyrant against truth? It is almost as if the steady flux of time was interrupted centuries ago, by some momentous—or trivial—event, and we have been left stranded like fish upon the beach of progress, with no sense of direction and little hope of achieving a better world. There has been a darkness upon our world for centuries, Donella: have you never wondered if there will ever be a renaissance, a true flowering of all that is best in mankind? Donella, listen to me—if Galileo is right, then *somewhere there is a better world than this.*"

Her dull eyes stared back. "Or a worse one."

He let his hands drop slowly from her shoulders, a dazed look in his eyes. "But. . . of course. How stupid of me to

121

forget. A *multitude* of possible worlds.. . ."

Donella shrugged and looked wistful. "All that may be so, Conrad. But this is the only world *we* have, and we had best make the most of it. That is how my father would put it."

But Conrad was far away in thought; she could tell from the intense expression in his eyes. She could almost hear his mind at work, turning this way and that the perplexing problem he had been left to solve.

Afterwards, she would remember that her action had not been entirely impulsive, but rather an outcome of all that had been growing between them, from that first night in Mallory's house when they had faced each other in the flickering lamplight.

While he was still deep in thought, she reached out and gently placed her hands upon his cheeks and turned his head to face her. His eyes wore a puzzled expression; they seemed only to half-see her.

She leaned forward and kissed him.

It was a deep kiss; it caught him by surprise. And while her own lips lingered lovingly, his were too stunned to respond.

It lasted but a moment. By the time he realized what had happened and reached out to hold her, his hands grasped only the void where she had been.

She stood up quickly and stepped back, a smile upon her lips, a lingering sadness in her dark eyes. "I'll call you when breakfast is ready," she said softly. And without another word she was gone.

He was left alone with only the company of horses and a fever on his lips and the air still vibrant with her presence.

T E N

The hinges of heaven

Conrad sat in a daze for some time before he willed himself
to move. He stood up and walked over to his saddle, kneeling down to replace his pocket-book in its pouch. From then
on his actions became almost automatic; his mind refused to
think coherently. He lifted the saddle and hoisted it rather
clumsily across the back of his mare.

His thoughts revolved around the ragged little urchin who
had kissed him. No girl had ever before kissed him with such
feeling. Oh, he knew well enough the playful pecks of village
girls, and the coarse, unfeeling kisses of tavern wenches. But
Donella's lips had been. . . different. They had passed on to
him an affection such as he had never known before.

How had Asquith spoken of her? *As one who had been
made a woman before she had finished with being a child.*
The remark had puzzled him at the time, but now he understood what his Master had gently implied.

Donella had kissed him as a warm and loving woman. *And
how did I respond?* he wondered, realizing that there had
scarcely been time for him to have acquitted himself at all
well. But her smile as she left him expressed no disappoint-
ment; she must have known how surprised he would be.

Slowly the fever faded from his lips, leaving behind only a
lingering memory. His mind wandered, roaming a rich
tapestry of possibilities. He imagined her properly attired in
the manner to which she had been born: wearing long,
brocaded gowns and fine slippers on her tiny feet, and with
her dark hair long and braided—no! flowing freely in the

123

wind. This was how he imagined her best. Ah, it was a tragedy to see her and her father reduced to such penury.

It was with his mind still fixed upon such matters that he led his horse outside. He squinted against the newly risen sun and saw the cordon of soldiers strung out along the shore of the lake, and the cavalry keeping guard around the perimeter; there were even some horsemen visible high along the rim of the valley.

It was quiet in the township; only a faint murmur of voices drifted over to him, in contrast to the rowdy conversation of the soldiers. No one moved on the no-man's land between the lake and the township. It was still too early for the people to gauge the temper of the Duke's men; they had no idea what the day would bring forth.

Conrad frowned. The prospect of riding out to investigate his markers on the north and south flanks of The Wall seemed a dangerous undertaking. Of course he had a story prepared if one of the horse-soldiers challenged him: he would explain that he was staying at the monastery, and that Brother Anselmo would speak for him. This would no doubt save any unpleasantness, but would at the same time serve to get him back into that place and bring an end to his studies. So what should he do?

His ability to think out his problem was not helped by his preoccupation with Donella; the warmth of her presence, the touching sadness of her beauty constantly interfered with his thinking.

In desperation he looked up at the looming face of The Wall. The sunlight had by now obscured the fine network of lines that stood out so clearly before sunrise, but the outward curvature was still pronounced. And even the soldiers seemed concerned by the rapid advance of the waters overnight, gauging by the odd comments that drifted over to him.

"Conrad!"

He turned slowly around. Donella was standing only a few paces away; a worried expression had driven away her lingering happiness.

"You're not riding out today, are you?" she asked, her voice filled with concern.

He looked confused, uncertain. "I. . . I'm not sure what I should do. Donella. . . *help me*!" For the first time since he had arrived in the valley *he did not know what to do*.

She took his hand. "Leave your horse. Come inside and have breakfast with us. That will give you time to think and decide what needs to be done. . ."

He nodded. Hers was a wise suggestion. He looped the reins of his horse over the barn door and went with her.

de Vargas was seated at the table, a bowl of gruel before him. He looked up when they entered, aiming his sightless eyes in the direction of the bright rectangle he knew to be the open doorway. "Good morning, Conrad," he said, sounding unusually jolly and firmer in voice than ever before; no doubt his restful night had done him some good. "Sit down, join us. Donella will see to it that you have something to eat."

Conrad sat down opposite the blind knight. Donella flashed him a smile and gently touched his cheek. And this time neither felt any embarrassment at this exchange of feeling, for a deep and abiding affection had been forged between them. It was the strangest emotion he had ever known. . . and the most powerful. For Donella it was a relief from years of hopeless bondage to an inhospitable world: she had finally found someone she could trust. . . and admire.

"Tell me," de Vargas went on, spooning up his gruel, "how goes yonder Wall this morning, eh?"

In a flat voice Conrad detailed how the lake had advanced and how the phenomenon seemed to have grown accordingly. "But I have not yet measured it," he said, defensively. And went on to explain how the Duke's soldiers maintained their cordon and patrolled all around the lake, how still the township was, how deathly quiet the land that separated these opposing forces. He said nothing of the theory he had

125

advanced of how The Wall might have been formed, and he knew Donella would not betray his trust. This was knowledge that would only serve to confuse her father, because he lacked the ability actually to *see* the phenomenon and the effects it had brought about: all he had to go by were words—his and the girl's.

Donella laid a plate before him; on it was a piece of dry sausage and a slice of bread. But it was sustenance; he smiled and thanked her. A second cup of herb tea was soon placed beside the plate; the sweet aroma jostled his thoughts and brought back the memory of their magic time together.

He looked up. But Donella only gave him a impish smile and moved away, attending to her chores.

The student frowned. He looked across at de Vargas, who had by now finished his gruel and was sipping noisily at his tea.

"There is a matter that bothers me greatly," the boy began, hesitantly. "It is the safety of yourself and your daughter. . and of Hakim. Mallory is another matter; I will speak with the old shepherd when I find him. I know that he is even now secreting his small flock in the gully where the creek runs, but he will need to take them to higher ground ere long."

The blind knight gave him a long, blank stare. "Why say you so, Conrad?"

"Because of the lake, my lord. The nature of The Wall I cannot predict, but that the lake is spreading cannot be denied. I fear that in another few days—probably less— this entire valley may be awash. So it is for your own safety that I urge you to leave this place and—"

"Go where?" de Vargas interjected. "To the monastery?" He almost spat the words. "Well, there might have been a chance at one time, if only for the safety of my daughter. But that opportunity is now long past, Conrad: would you have me entrust her safety to a place overrun with royal rabble? The worthy brothers will have their work cut

126

out as it is, without having to keep watch over Donella. For myself, I care little; but for my daughter I would give all I have. You understand?''

Conrad nodded, out of habit. ''If this be so, then take her from this valley, before it is too late. You know the lake is advancing—''

''I do not question your wisdom in that matter, Conrad.''

''Well then, do you intend to remain here until its waters are lapping through the doorway?''

de Vargas said soberly, ''Perhaps. But mark you this: I will not be made to move. That would take some doing.'' For a moment it seemed that genuine fire flashed in his dead eyes.

The boy looked across at Donella. She shook her head, cautioning him not to pursue the matter further. Exasperated, he spread his arms in a gesture of defeat.

''As you will, then,'' he said, He pushed aside the plate of food and left it untouched. He stood up. ''Thank you again for your hospitality.'' But there was a bitter taste on his palate. And some of his displeasure must have crept into his words, for the blind knight suddenly softened in his manner.

''Conrad,'' he said, ''I value your counsel. More: we have come to think of you as one of our own, as a friend. Why then so gloomy, eh?'' His intuition had accurately gauged the boy's state of mind.

''It is . . . nothing,'' Conrad lied. This did not come easy—but how could he explain his confused state of mind, created by his burgeoning love for de Vargas' daughter and his fear of what might happen in the valley? ''Now, if you will excuse me, I will look for Mallory. He, too, must be warned.''

He nodded politely to Donella, feeling a sharp pain in his breast as he did so. She simply bowed her head, unable to face him.

The boy went outside, shouldering his newly found burden of grief and joy. Joy and grief. *Oh, Asquith, Asquith!*

Where are you now when I so desparetely need you?

He paused just outside the doorway, gave a cursory nod to Hakim, then looked out over the valley towards the lake. Already there was some activity around the hastily constructed dais. Some people had even wandered cautiously from the township and gathered before the shrine, wondering if the promised services would take place. The majority of them must be genuinely devout, the student realized, otherwise they would not have risked the wrath of the soldiers. But a general air of tranquillity had overtaken the proceedings, as though the hideous events of the previous day were already forgotten.

There was a long cavalcade winding down into the valley. The sunlight picked out the faded colours of many royal coaches, their pennants lack-lustre and drooping , and horsemen and people on foot. The majority of these were monks; he could distinguish their solemn garb from the faded finery of the noblemen.

He felt a gentle touch upon his arm. Without turning around he sensed who was standing beside him.

"Forgive my father," Donella said quietly. "He is often. . . stubborn. Do not doubt for one moment that he appreciates the wisdom of your advice, but alas. . ." She shrugged. "It is just that he cannot bring himself to do as you suggest. He would like, if he could, to find another way out."

"My lady," he whispered, this form of address falling simply and naturally to his lips, "there may be no alternative." He turned to face her. "Do your best to convince him to move from this place. There may not be much time left for him to delay a safe course of action." Almost abruptly, he made to move off.

"Wait." She caught at his arm; held him fast. "Where are you going? Surely—"

He smiled. "No, I have decided it would be unwise to explore the valley on horseback. Instead I will mingle with the people already crowded around the dais. I have a mind to witness whatever elaborate service our Abbot has prepared for us."

There was a touch of desperation in her dark eyes. "You will take care?"

"Of course. My good Master has taught me how to hide myself among a crowd, even if it be of the enemy camp."

An aching void seemed to separate them. But it would have been premature to have even tried to fill it. Patience and time would bring them closer together; of that he felt sure. For the time being there was work to be done.

He took her hand, kissed it briefly, and said softly, "And *you* take care, my lady."

She nodded, and withdrew her hand. And with a deep sense of foreboding watched him march off in the direction of the lake.

● ● ●

More people were beginning to emerge from their ramshackle dwellings and tents, their courage affirmed by the presence of so many of their numbers standing unmolested around the dais. Conrad joined them, assuming a humble manner. No one questioned his presence: with few exceptions they were all strangers to one another in this strange valley.

The crowd stood three-deep before the wooden shrine. The student managed to find himself a place in the second row. The cordon of soldiers kept a careful eye upon the crowd; a half a dozen cavalry rode around it, alert for any show of force. But it soon became apparent that this was a chastened group and that there need be no cause for further action—unless one of their number chose to run amok for some reason, in which case he would be quickly cut down before his example could incite others.

Conrad kept a careful eye upon the numbers building up around and behind him, in case the need for sudden flight should arise. But for the most part his attention was held by the wooden shrine directly in front of the crowd.

He was surprised to see how effectively the monks had transformed the jury-rigged dais. High framework had been rigged on either side to support a number or beautiful tapestries and other holy cloths brought from the monastery. The front of the dais had been left open so that the necessary services might be performed there, but at the back. . .

Never before had the student seen such a magnificent carving of the Child on the Wheel. Whatever unknown craftsman had worked that huge piece of wood had done so with the inspiration of a great artist and the soul of a religious zealot. This replica of the Child Martyr, who had died when he was only a year or so younger than Conrad, was uncomfortably lifelike. His outstretched limbs, spread-eagled and nailed to the Wheel, aroused a macabre feeling in the boy. The Seven Arrows that pierced His naked breast had been fashioned with a dedicated attention to detail. The agony depicted on His face was astonishingly vivid: staring eyes and slack jaw, and pain etched in every inch of His face.

Conrad felt his mouth go dry and his heart beat faster. This image—and hundreds more like it—had haunted him nearly all his life: a carven idol of a fourteen-year-old messiah who had been brutally murdered almost seventeen hundred years ago.

Perhaps that was when the great darkness descended upon our world, he mused, recalling his conversation with Donella. That could have been the vital point in time when history had gone awry, and the Church that had arisen, like a phoenix, from the dark deed of His murder, had established a tyranny when it might instead have become just and good.

But all this will change, he thought. *And we, the Scientists of this world, will rekindle the light of reason and intellect and shatter the iron fist of ignorance which the Church has closed around mankind.* So ran his dream, which was also the dream of countless others, who, like himself, worked under the shadow of the tyrant.

He lifted his gaze. Behind this elaborately carved idol, The Wall reared up into the sky, shedding a bright and benevolent light over the proceedings. It made a magnificent backdrop.

• • •

A while later the vanguard of the descending cavalcade stopped just short of the dais. Behind the coaches a long line of monks and sightseers stretched out and up to the entrance to the valley, where hundreds more could be seen watching from a distance.

The Abbot arrived in the Duke's coach, with the old patriach grumbling beside him and scowling through the window at the crowd.

His officers deployed a fresh company of twelve cavalrymen in a wide arc before the shrine. A few gentle passes with their lowered lances ensured that the crowd moved back several paces. The student shuffled with them.

When the Duke was satisfied that enough distance had been established between himself and these people, he gave further instructions. Trumpets blew a fanfare. Another group of cavalrymen galloped off towards the township to make sure no stragglers remained, that every one was in attendance before the dais. When this was accomplished, roughly two hundred people stood a trifle uneasily before the shrine. Not all had come willingly; some had sullen faces and muttered darkly under their breath, but they knew better than to go against the Duke's wishes. . . and his watchful soldiers.

With solemn dignity the Abbot stepped forth from the Duke's royal coach. He wore his finest red robes and his Seal of Office: a large silver emblem of the Wheel strung about his neck, resting against his chest. He moved on to the dais and took up his position at the very centre, with an archer on either side. He turned to face the crowd.

The Duke waited until a sedan chair arrived; then he was carried on to the dais with customary ritual. His chair was set down on the Abbot's left, where he surveyed the 'congregation' with a surly indifference. Such close proximity to the rabble always unnerved him: he knew that they could very easily rob him of all he possessed if the balance of power ever shifted in their favour; such was the nature of the world. But first they would need a leader, and none had been detected by his spies among this rough assortment of mankind. So he surveyed them with disdain, and hoped that the Abbot would not be too long-winded with his speech. Meanwhile, he fidgeted and fanned his leathery cheeks with a fan; the waves of heat and humidity coming from The Wall were most unpleasant. He hoped this farce would soon be over, so that they could get down to business. The Abbot had convinced him that his presence was necessary at this historic moment, and of course he was right: the Church was often more far-sighted in matters of civil strategy. To have the Duke of Bloyne at his side would place a royal seal upon all that would follow.

But the wily Abbot bided his time. He was not in any hurry; it served his particular purpose to have his congregation wait and gape. Only when the last of them had been sent scurrying to join the others crowded before the dais did he begin his oration.

He chose his moment skilfully. He waited until the sun had just begun to move down behind The Wall and the valley was bathed in supernal light.

He began with a simple preamble. He reminded the people assembled before him of the nature of their God, Whose Child had died upon the Wheel. And when he was confident that he held their attention, he launched eagerly into the speech which he had laboured upon the whole of the previous evening.

"Oh, my brothers—this Wall you see is indeed a miracle wrought by His own hands: a Sign which He has sent us in our time of crisis. Never before have we been privileged to see such divine evidence of His presence in our lives—here, *in our valley*." The Abbot placed a particular stress upon these words. "It is a wonder such as the world has never seen before, and may never see again. It is His way of letting us know that we have not been forgotten, that the ugly spectres of drought and pestilence will soon disappear from our land, and we will embark upon a golden age of prosperity. This much has He promised me, for the Lord God came to me in a vision and told me of these wonders. . . and others which will follow. Listen. . ." And he proceeded to give them details of the 'miraculous qualities' of the lake water; how it might cure the sick and lame and people with all kinds of ills, but only if they believed and if their souls were properly cleansed.

Conrad was impressed by his zealous delivery and surprised that such a powerful and authoritative voice could emerge from so frail a body. But he reminded himself that the Abbot was a man possessed by a private vision, which he was unlikely to divulge to his congregation, because it involved the sin of avarice. Yet the student did not allow any cynicism to show on his face; he maintained a look of pious innocence throughout the long proceedings.

"Now, brothers—let us pray. Here, by the waters He has sent us, and below the glory He has brought with them. Let us give thanks and may the Almighty hear our voices, for this is indeed a wondrous miracle He has visited upon us. . ."

Every head bowed in accord with his command. Some even knelt on the muddy ground and clasped their hands in readiness. Even the Duke's soldiers lowered their heads, although a few peered through half-closed lids, as they had been directed, in order to maintain their vigil.

The Abbot led his motley congregation in a short Adoration followed by an extended Prayer. He felt he could afford to be lavish in his worship, when he considered the worldly boon that would soon be his. A volley of 'amens' echoed across the valley.

The Abbot stood with his legs braced wide-apart, his arms uplifted. "Now hear me!" he thundered. "Let it be known to each one of you that I have consecrated these waters, in the name of God and his Child, who died upon the Wheel." With a sweep of his right arm he directed the attention of the crowd to the carven image behind him. "No man, woman or child may enter this lake, or partake of its waters, unless they have first delivered themselves unto God by proper baptism. Therefore, if there be sinners or athiests among you, now is the time to be absolved of your follies. For whomsoever bathes in these miraculous waters shall be deemed fortunate in the eyes of God and all mankind. . ."

Miraculous. The word was quickly taken up and spread through the crowd like a wave. The soldiers tensed, but there was no sign that there would be a repetition of the previous day's fiasco.

Miraculous. . .

It was only through a great effort that the Abbot was able to withhold a smile of contempt. He considered that he had delivered his master-stroke with superb artistry and that he held his audience in the palm of his hand; he gloried in his triumph. Everything else had ceased to matter: only worldly success concerned him now.

The Duke was bored. He had sat stiffly throughout the Abbot's diatribe, letting his mind consider the financial prospects of their arrangements. They had already reached agreement on the price of the casks of lake water, but the toll arrangements needed more thought. A booth placed at the very entrance to the valley, to ensure that no fool got a free look at this miracle.—Yes, that was something he would have to work on. . . .

". . . baptisms will begin almost immediately," the Abbot was saying, obviously enjoying the sound of his own voice. "I will officiate over the first, as promised, and from time to time thereafter. But Brother Anselmo will be in charge at all other times: it is to him you will need to look for guidance when I am not present. Now, let us bow our heads once more in final prayer before we begin.''

"*Show me*!" A roar came from the back of the crowd, and a ripple of shock passed through the reluctant congregation. Even Conrad's heart gave a sudden leap, for he recognized that voice. . .

"*Show me*!" roared the same voice. "Let me see your miracle of water, Sir Abbot! Explain why you have taken it upon yourself to claim this lake in the name of the Church! I find precious little to accept in your talk of a 'vision'. Make way! Make way for a knight of the realm!"

Dear God, the boy thought, *It is de Vargas. .!*

"Yes!" cried another bold voice. "Make way for a knight of the realm. . ."

As if by some subtle form of magic, an opening appeared in the crowd. The student turned around; sure enough, there was the familiar figure of the blind knight striding forward, with Hakim at his side and his daughter a little to the rear, a wretched look upon her face.

For a moment the boy was too paralyzed to move. The Abbot on the dais, too, was transfixed by surprise.

"My lord!" Conrad called out at last as de Vargas drew level; but the blind knight either did not or chose not to hear him. He strode by, led by his faithful squire.

Stunned by this unexpected turn of events, Conrad still had enough presence of mind to grasp the girl's arm as she walked past and pull her roughly to him. *"Donella!"* he whispered hoarsly. "What is he doing?"

It took a moment for his voice to register, for her even to recognize him, so clouded was her mind with fear. She collapsed against him. "Oh, Conrad, I could not keep him away. He *wanted* to come. . .''

"''Go no farther," he said, taking firm hold of her. "Stay here, with me, until this thing has run its course." He could not know that it would end in tragedy, but somehow he sensed that it might.

• • •

The blind knight came to a halt before the dais. Hakim stood to his right, eyeing the crowd and the soldiers with professional skill.

"I am Ramon de Vargas," the knight announced, "a knight of this realm. As my lord Abbot can observe, I am blind. I was made blind in the course of fighting God's war with the heathen Slavs. Will these waters cleanse my eyes, Sir Abbot, so that I may see again?"

The Abbot regarded him cautiously, and chose his words with care. "If indeed thy soul be pure, and thy heart be—"

"God damn thee, man!" de Vargas cried. "Did you not hear me? *I have fought God's war!* Whose heart could be pure after what I have seen, while you and all your kind remained cloistered? I ask you again, will these waters give me back my sight?"

It was a touchy moment. For once the Abbot was caught off-guard, without a prepared reply. And his hesitancy angered de Vargas still further.

"You are silent, my lord Abbot." Behind, the crowd grew restless; the soldiers eyed the mob uneasily. They did not want a repetition of the previous day's massacre. "Tell me then, if God has truly spoken to you—and I sincerely doubt it—by what right have you taken it upon yourself to assume control of these waters, when, if God be just, they should belong to all mankind?"

The Abbot paled. He looked anxiously to the Duke for some sign of support. The Duke merely made a gesture with his fan, indicating that this was entirely the Abbot's responsibility.

"My lord Abbot!" de Vargas cried. "I say that you lie, that you make a mockery of the God you espouse, that you—"

Afterwards, no one would be certain what had precipitated

136

the action. Perhaps it was an archer who mistook one of the Duke's languid gestures as a direction. But before de Vargas had finished his accusation there was a sudden *swish!* of a shaft released from a crossbow.

It took the blind knight from behind, passing through his back and emerging from his chest. de Vargas staggered, coughed, and almost collapsed; but somehow he managed to keep his feet for a moment longer. He clutched at the edge of the dais, a stunned expression on his ruined face. A great moan went up from the crowd. The cavalry surged forward, lances dipped and at the ready. The archers aimed their crossbows. The man who had released the untimely shaft carefully rewound and refitted his bow, as if nothing had happened.

de Vargas slipped and fell to the ground. He rolled over on his back and felt a great pain in his chest. . . but also a kind of peace: at last. For in the moment before he died he *saw.* The shock of the crossbow shaft had shaken him free of the thrall which had bound his sight these many long years. His vision cleared: he saw The Wall burning brightly overhead, and when he let his head roll to one side, he saw it reaching out to the farthest rim of the valley. It was a glory such as he could never have believed possible; no matter how eloquent had been his daughter's descriptions, they could not match what he now *saw.* . . with his dying eyes.

"Dear. . . God," he managed to say, blood gushing from his mouth. "I have seen You. . . at last." Then his eyes glazed over in death.

A guttural cry rose up from the crowd. It came from only one throat and seemed scarcely human: it was the only sound that the mute and towering Hakim could dredge up. Its impact was terrifying. Surging forward, he drew his enormous broadsword and struck forward in the direction of the Abbot.

Donella screamed. Conrad had the presence of mind to place one hand firmly over her mouth, to stifle her cry, while

with the other hand he dragged her back through the crowd pressing forward. "Donella," he whispered, "there is nothing we can do—*nothing*." But all the while she struggled against him, biting deep into his hand until the blood flowed, her eyes rolling wildly. The pain in his hand was frightful, yet he endured it; and gradually he drew them back through the crowd into the open land.

The Saracen put up a brave fight: that much at least Conrad saw. He took a dozen shafts before he began to slow down, and more than a dozen of the Duke's best men were killed before the giant was subdued.

"Help me, Donella!" the boy begged. "We must save ourselves and I cannot do it alone!"

Gradually his words got through to her and she ceased to struggle. Together they stumbled away from the crowd, heading towards they knew not what.

The Abbot was shocked by what had happened. He had expected some small criticisms, but nothing quite like this. And the Duke. . . the Duke was busy fanning himself and disclaiming all responsibility for what had happened. Yet eighteen men lay dead at his feet.

And at that precise moment of indecision there came a great groaning noise overhead. It was as though the very hinges of Heaven had been put under a great strain: the earth shook and the sky reverberated to a rolling thunder unlike anything ever heard before.

The Wall bulged outwards over the lake. And the network of fissures, which before had seemed so elusive, were suddenly revealed as stark and ominous. Then there came a gigantic report, like several cracks of thunder rolled in to one; and wide rivulets of water began to pour down into the lake from the fissures.

The Duke was awed and frightened by this display. He quickly summoned his attendants and they lifted his chair and took him back to his coach. He paused only long enough to remark, with an almost casual lack of concern: "It seems you have angered your God, my lord Abbot. I suggest you had best appease him. . . as quickly as possible.'' Then he gestured to his underlings to bear him away.

Dazed, the Abbot could only gaze in wonder and apprehension at the sudden transformation of The Wall. The sky still carried the resounding echo and the ground underfoot still shuddered from the impact of the dreadful thunder.

He wrung his hands and cursed his ill-fortune. The event could not have been more ill-timed; already his newly won congregation was falling back from the dais. There was fear stamped on the face of every one of them; and they had been shocked by the death of the courageous knight and his squire. One thing was sure: there would be no baptisms today.

●　●　●

Conrad and Donella found their way safely back to Mallory's house. And there they remained, watching from afar the retreat of the Abbot and his underlings, and all the Duke's entourage: only his cordon of soldiers were left behind, and it was obvious that they had no liking for their task. The last of the 'congregation' hurried back to join their companions in the township, and there they huddled throughout the long afternoon, marking the frightening changes that were taking place on The Wall.

At sunset it blazed like a great scar on the heavens, the dark fissures brought out boldly by the setting sun. So menacing did this seem at close-range that the soldiers turned their backs upon it, lest it addle their wits.

Conrad marked all this with interest, but to Donella it hardly mattered. There was space in her mind only for her father's death, and for the great yawning loneliness that faced her.

Conrad understood this. He held her close until the last of her tears had been shed and her body had ceased to shake; then only dull, dry grief was left and she leaned her soft

141

weight against him like a ghost.

Thus they stayed together throughout the long and lonely night, while Mallory and his dog tossed restlessly by the fireside and the dreadful scar finally faded from the sky and was replaced by a gossamer innocence.

And in the morning there was a foul breath upon the land.

ELEVEN

Retreat from the valley

The boy was roused from his deep sleep by a rough shaking of his shoulder. He opened his eyes and saw the old shepherd bending over him. There was a worried look in Mallory's watery eyes and a suggestion of desperation.

"Forgive me for waking you so soon," he apologized. "But as you can well see, my young lord, the day is well on its way—and so must I be. I've take yer advice and be movin' my sheep to higher ground. But I did not want to leave without lettin' you know where I be. If you need me, look for me on yonder western slopes. The grazing there is not too bad. Meantime, treat this house as yer own while I am gone." And without another word he was left, leaving the door slightly ajar so that brilliant sunlight poured in.

The boy was still only half-awake; slowly he came to his senses. Two things hastened this: the quality of the sunlight, which indicated how far the morning had advanced, and an incredibly bad odour that almost made him gag on his first few breaths. The house was filled with the disgusting stench; it reminded him of every foul waterway he had ever known, every filthy dockside he had ever visited. It was the rank and overpowering odour of decayed matter.

Even as he fought back the rising waves of nausea he grew aware of a weight pressing down upon his left shoulder. Without sitting up in bed he turned his face around and saw Donella's pale face resting against him, still locked in her own deep sleep. Dimly he recalled how they had both drifted off to sleep in the early hours of the morning; they had lain

143

together, without any coverings, drawing warmth form each other through their closeness.

He remembered the way her father had died and repressed a grim shudder. And he felt a fleeting sadness for the mighty Saracen, who had died so valiantly yet in such a futile manner. But his face set in a grim smile when he recalled the carnage around the shrine and the number of soldiers Hakim had taken with him before they cut him down.

His mind became more alert as more and more details crowded his waking mind: the sudden groaning of the heavens, The Wall bulging forward, the fine network of fissures revealed as wide cracks in the face of the phenomenon; the fear that had spread like a wave through the Abbot's hastily assembled congregation and their gradual retreat from the dais to their little township. . . the Abbot's decision to postpone further ceremonies and his own hasty departure, along with the Duke's entourage. *But why this awful odour?*

Carefully he disengaged himself from the sleeping girl—he did not wish to disturb her from her much-needed rest—and made his way to the open door. But even before he reached it he could hear cries of consternation outside, from the direction of the township. And when he stepped outside he could well appreciate their cause.

It was mid-morning. Overnight the lake had advanced an enormous distance; the wooden shrine stood as a small island a short distance from the shore. The water was badly discoloured; a breeze stirred up wavelets and sent them scurrying towards the shore, carrying the fetid odour which had spread throughout the valley. Several monks were wading around the dais, cassocks hitched high, the water swirling around their calves. They were trying to salvage the valuable icons and tapestries which they had brought down from the monastery. It appeared that they were having little success, for the wooden platform rocked about like a raft on the discoloured surface of the lake.

144

Conrad looked up at The Wall. This morning not even the fiery sun could mask its mottled face, and the wide fissures from which a rank, dark sediment oozed and flowed down into the lake. The boy's nose wrinkled in disgust. Here, then, was the source of the unbelievably foul odour that filled the valley.

The Wall was no longer a vision of aching supernatural beauty; it looked more like a scabrous, weeping wound suspended in the sky, as though this portion of space and time had acquired a sickness.

The ground was moist underfoot. Only a few paces away from the house it was already awash with seepage from the swollen lake. No wonder Mallory had decided to make his move: it was doubtful whether his house would be habitable by the end of the day.

Conrad's thoughts returned to Donella: what was to become of her? More to the point, what was to become of them both? They would have to abandon the shepherd's house; that much was obvious. Then what? The chances of being well received at the monastery were remote at this stage; he could not rely on Brother Anselmo to remember a bargain made in coin when so much had happened in between, nor to help protect a girl of whom he knew nothing.

After some consideration he decided it would be best to take her with him to Abingdon, where good friends would take care of her. But that would mean leaving the site of all these strange happenings straight away. They would not be able to travel as fast as Master Asquith. With luck they might meet up with the Scientist returning to the valley, in which case only a day or so at the most would have been lost to scientific observation—and surely Asquith would understand?

The boy was torn two ways. By his loyalty to the College and the Oath he had sworn to Science; and by his deep feelings for the girl and for her safety. Fortunately for him the remembered words of a sage helped him out of this dilemma:

145

'The oath that you don't take is often more binding than the one you do.'

A great warmth filled his heart and for a moment he forgot the foul stench that filled the valley and relived some of the wonderful moments he had shared with Donella. . . as well as the sadness.

The monks continued their struggle with the rocking, shifting dais. The cordon of soldiers had fallen back several hundred yards and were clustered in angry groups, muttering among themselves. There was no sign of any cavalry; they were the last of the Duke's men left in the valley, and it was obvious that they did not relish their posting.

A sudden sound made Conrad whirl around and hasten back into the house.

Donella was sitting up on the bed, a hand raised to cover the bottom half of her face, a wild look in her eyes. It was apparent to him that she was trying to fight back the first waves of nausea she had encountered when she woke.

Relief washed over her when she saw him. She dropped her hand. "Conrad? What is it? What is that awful—"

He hastened over and took her gently in his arms, stroking her hair while he told her not to panic. "It is just some new thing The Wall has put forth. . ." And he told her of the foul ooze pouring down into the lake, and the effect it was having upon the soldiers and the people camped about the township. Already some of them were dismantling their crude shelters or collapsing their tents and getting ready to move to higher ground where they hoped the stench would not be so overpowering.

Suddenly her body stiffened in his embrace. Without looking up, she said in a hollow voice, muffled against his chest, "Is this real? Did everything happen. . . as I remember it now?"

He said gently, "I fear so, my lady." This form of address now seemed to him most natural. He no longer felt himself to be the shy, innocent boy who had entered the valley—and yet not quite a man, either. He could not quite fathom the

146

change in himself. "Your father is dead, but he died honourably," he told Donella gently. "I was close enough to hear his last words: I believe that for a few moments, before he died, his sight was restored.—Yes, Donella, perhaps it was as I thought: perhaps the shock of the arrow shaft shattered the veil cast over his eyes—that, or the sudden realization that he was about to die. But he did *see,* for I heard him cry out to the Lord that he had *seen The Wall.* I believe that it was for this reason that he may have died happy; I certainly wish it so, for he was a fine and noble man."

"And Hakim?"

His face lit up. "Ah, if you could have seen him, Donella!—But you were too busy struggling with me as I tried to drag you away from the danger point. But he fought valiantly and died with honour. Why, he must have taken a dozen or more of the Duke's men before they finally slew him. . ."

Then he went on to remind her of the sudden change that had taken place in The Wall: how the heavens had groaned and the great fissures had appeared for all to see; how a mighty thunder had echoed across the sky and the ground underneath their feet had shuddered, throwing many people off their balance. How rivers of water had sprung from the fissures in The Wall and poured down into the lake, and how the Abbot and his underlings, along with the Duke's entourage, had been forced to withdraw from the valley and the rest of the people back to their township.

"Only a few soldiers remain," he finished, "and from their surly looks I do not think they will remain for long—not when their companions are enjoying the comparative luxury of the monastery." He stood up, holding her at arm's length. "And we too must leave. By afternoon this house will be awash. The old shepherd has already gone: he has taken his flock to the western slopes."

She looked up at him with a haggard, desperate expression. "But *where* will we go, Conrad? Where will we be safe? The monastery will not take us in. . ."

"Donella. . ." He took a deep breath and let go of her, then clasped his hands behind his back and did his best to look like someone capable of making important decisions. "My work should continue here until my Master returns. But that is still several days distant. In the meantime, it is your safety that concerns me. Now, I have devised a scheme whereby you will accompany me back to Abingdon—"

"But if you leave your post, what will your Master say?" she interjected, obviously concerned as much for him as he was for her.

"If we are fortunate, we will meet up with my Master on his way back from the College, in which case only a day or so will have been lost from our Record. If not. . ." He shrugged. By now it was apparent even to Donella where his first loyalty lay, and she was deeply touched.

"But what will happen to me when we reach your Abingdon?" she asked quietly.

"Happen? Why, I have many good friends in Abingdon who will take care of you until I return. They will see that you have fine clothes such as befit a girl of your station, and they will help you to forget these dreadful past years. . ."

Her eyes filled with tears. She stood up and faced him, with half a pace between them. She wrapped her hands loosely around his neck and looked him squarely in the eyes, her bottom lip trembling. "Conrad, you cannot know. . . you should know that—"

He took her sorry face between his hands and said with soft severity, "Donella, there is nothing I need to know of you that I do not already know. The rest is past, and most of it little more than a bad dream. Your life will have a new beginning, you understand? It does not do to dwell upon the past, not even its more pleasant aspects. Life moves forward, never back, if it is to grow. And you *will* grow, Donella."

For a long time they stared into each other's eyes, locked

together by the deep feelings they shared. Then slowly he released his hands, unwound hers from around his neck, and stood back.

The girl nodded. "I will do as you wish. I will come with you to Abingdon. Your friends there . . . you make them sound so kind and gracious."

"And that they be, my lady: kind and generous spirits, every one of them. You will find no riff-raff in our College town. . ."

Oh, Conrad, she thought, *whatever would I have done without you?* But it was not necessary for her to put these thoughts into words; an understanding passed silently between them that did away with any need to express gratitude.

The boy walked to the door and looked out. He noticed that several of the Duke's cavalry had joined the cordon of soldiers, and that they were engaged in heated argument. This came to an abrupt halt when the horse soldiers wheeled their mounts away and galloped off and up the rutted path leading out of the valley. After some short consultation among themselves, the foot soldiers formed disorderly ranks and set off after them.

Now at last Conrad saw his chance. But now the morning breeze had been stirred into a light wind; it pushed the fetid odour of the lake and The Wall into every nook and cranny in the valley. The stench was so overwhelming that Conrad almost vomited. No wonder the soldiers had refused to stay.

He staggered back inside, overcome for the moment by the foul fumes. "Donella," he managed to say. "Before we leave. . . there is an opportunity for me to do a little close study of The Wall. The soldiers have gone, driven off by this dreadful stench. Now, I will saddle two horses, for I would not have you waiting here alone. And if you could fashion some heavy face-masks from a blanket? I think we will need them if we are to withstand the air outside—even more so when we are close to The Wall itself. . ."

149

The girl nodded. "Of course, Conrad. But don't you think we should first have something to eat?"

The boy shook his head. "I doubt if I could hold down any food, my lady. That stench. . ."

"Then at least some tea, before you set off?" she suggested.

A lingering smile passed between them. "Do you have enough herbs left?" he asked.

"I think so." And she set about the task, the fetid air forgotten while her mind dwelt dreamily upon the moment when they had first discovered their love. . .

●　　●　　●

The monastery seethed with unrest. The light but purposeful wind had wafted the unpleasant odour even this far afield, and even though it lacked the overpowering stench that had caused many of the Duke's soldiers in the valley to throw up their guts, it was still powerful enough to offend.

The Abbot raged in silence, moving around his grounds, sensing the growing hostility within the monastery walls, and carrying the dead-weight of his dream of worldly wealth.

As the day grew more advanced the stench from the valley became even more offensive; many of the royal ladies swooned and even the faces of several soldiers paled against this unseen onslaught upon their senses. The portion of The Wall that loomed high above the valley seemed to leer at them with its cracked and mottled face; hastily people began to make the Sign of the Wheel on their breasts; for it now seemed to them that this so-called 'miracle' might not be God's work, but rather a prank played upon them by the great Adversary, the Devil Himself.

The Abbot was incensed to hear such rumours. He tried his best to suppress them, but to no avail; the idea had taken firm root and spread quickly through the swollen ranks crowded inside the monastery.

Already people had begun to move out of the valley; when

they found that they still did not escape the polluted air, they began to form angry clusters outside the monastery. It did not take them long to feed upon the fast-spreading rumour concerning the Devil. They fastened upon it with relish, half in fear, half in anger. More than anything else they felt cheated of the fine time they had been having, and when they cast about for a scapegoat, the Abbot of St Germaine came instantly to mind. After all, hadn't he tried to take over the valley and spoil their fun? Was it not he who summoned the Duke's soldiers and set them upon helpless bystanders? And hadn't he sought to claim the 'miraculous' waters of the lake, when, as the foolhardy old knight had insisted, they should belong to everyone?

They had only to look back at the scabrous face of The Wall to have their anger confirmed.

"Look!" one wit exclaimed, "heaven itself has the pox!" But only a faint ripple of laughter moved through the mob gathered outside the monastery walls; they were a surly, disappointed rabble, and their numbers swelled every moment as more and people deserted the fetid valley.

At first the Duke ignored these goings-on, but soon he grew disturbed by this strange turn of events. The foul odour hardly offended him; his olfactory senses had almost atrophied with age. But it bothered his men—particularly those left to maintain order in the valley. For a new contingent had been sent to replace that which had earlier deserted its post. The Duke listened attentively to his officers' advice, and finally had no choice but to agree: the soldiers must be recalled at once; they could not be expected to remain at their post under such dreadful conditions.

A group of cavalrymen rode off at once to inform the soldiers in the valley that they were recalled from duty. Meanwhile, the Duke retired to a secluded corner of the cloisters and sent word for the Abbot to join him. It was time to re-examine his commitments. He gave a deep sigh of regret when he realized that his dream of worldly wealth had not matured; now with most of the monastery's supplies consumed, it was time to be thinking about moving his court on to another more prosperous place where they might settle for a while. After all, neither his life nor his reputation depended on what happened here: that was the Abbot's sole concern. The Duke was not so old that he did not realize the safety of his soldiers and his court was his first concern. Everything else—even dreams—came second. He had ruled long enough to gauge the temper of his people, and he did not like the anger and hostility he sensed outside the monastery walls. Yes, it was time to be moving on. . .

The Abbot eventually joined him. He looked very old and very tired. "Sit down," said the Duke, motioning him to share a bench. "I have asked you here so that we may speak in privacy. I mean no offence, nor do any of my court. Broadly speaking, it seems your 'miracle' has turned foul upon us, my lord Abbot. Why, there is such a stench in the valley that I have been forced to summon the last of my soldiers from their post, and people are streaming away in droves—even the hucksters have packed up their stalls and are leaving!" He took a pinch of snuff from an elaborately jewelled box.

The Abbot shook his head. "I have nose enough to smell that stench, even here."

"Then you will understand why we must leave," the Duke said quickly. And then, more slowly—for the Abbot's face was filled with a dull puzzlement—"Because of this sudden change in—er, circumstances, I do not see how we can pursue our agreement to our mutual profit. You follow? There is talk of this being the Devil's own work—"

The Abbot nodded wearily. "I know. They are a credulous lot." *But what if they were right?* Could it be that he had had been mistaken. . . and been *duped?*

The Duke stood up. "Perhaps in time this disagreeable smell will waft itself away. If so, then I will rely on you let me know, so that I may return and perhaps resume our

152

arrangement.''

The Abbot did not seem to care one way or the other. The life seemed to have left his eyes; his spirit was lax. But suddenly he looked up: the Duke's words had finally penetrated. "You are not *leaving?*"

"I regret that I must, my lord Abbot. You have seen how restless my people have become: their noses are more sensitive than ours; they wish to be gone from this place—as quickly as possible. In all truth I cannot say that I blame them. But before we withdraw they must be fed, and our coaches provisioned, for we have a long journey ahead of us.''

The Duke wrapped his rich cloak tight around his shoulders and stared out into the crowd. Just then a sudden gust of wind brought the stench from the valley deep into his dull nostrils; he pulled a wry face. Then he marked the desperate plea in the Abbot's eyes and said softly, "You must work things out as best you can. It seems your Wall has turned out to be a bad omen, my friend: would that it were otherwise. But we must be moving on. If you could see to it that a modest lunch is prepared for my people—"

But the Abbot did not seem to hear him. He turned around, and, moving like a man in a trance, walked outside and pushed his way through the crowd in the direction of his lodge. Once inside he closed the door behind him and leaned against it, looking long and deeply into his personal tragedy.

The Duke did not waste time pondering the Abbot's strange behaviour. Quickly he summoned several of his officers, who soon set the hapless monks to work making the necessary preparations and arranging provisions for their journey. Then the Duke retired to his royal coach and brooded over all that might have been. . . As did the Abbot, alone in his eyrie overlooking the crowd.

● ● ●

The royal cavalcade moved out of the monastery shortly

153

after midday. When the tail-end of the court was safely out of sight, the angry crowd outside the walls suddenly surged in through the open gate. There was nothing the monks could do to stem this hostile tide of humanity from swarming through the grounds in search of food and wine.

The Abbot looked down from his window and groaned, burying his head in his hands. It was just as he had feared. Now that the restraining influence of the Duke's soldiers was no longer present there was nothing to stop this rabble from stripping the monastery bare. Robbed of their wretched 'miracle', they were sure to vent their fury upon anything and anyone they chose. God help the hapless monks. . .

The Abbot's teeth began to chatter; he could not stop them. A cold sweat broke out all over his body; a fever laid its hand upon his brow. He sank slowly to his knees, blotting out the sight of the angry mob below. His eyes glazed over, staring blankly ahead, while in his mind there burned the dreadful vision of The Wall in its present state of foul decay. When would the process end? Could this really be the work of the great Adversary—or had God chosen to mock and punish him for his avarice, and every other crime he had committed in the name of the Church? Ah, they were not so monstrous. . . but they were so *many*. . . and this last the worst of all!

His dream of a worldly empire had been shattered, and there was no way in which he could find consolation for his tormented soul. And so, gradually, and by devious means of self-delusion, his fragmented mind idled its way towards madness. . .

● ● ●

It was not long before the first riots broke out in the monastery. They began with a few fist-fights in the cellars, when thirsty knaves broke open what they thought were wine casks, only to discover them filled with water from the lake. In rage they turned upon each other and any unfortunate

154

monk who happened to be nearby. Most of these had the sense to cluster together in distant corners of the monastery, waiting for the wrath of the invaders to subside.

"Give us food! Give us wine!" roared the mob. These were no pious pilgrims but the very dregs of humanity, their senses overwhelmed by the foul odour reaching out from the valley. But there was no wine; there was no food: the Duke and his court had taken everything with them.

The roar of this angry mob finally brought the Abbot down from his eyrie. Some stubborn sense of purpose overcame his fear and he moved among them, trying to restore sense or order. But his voice was only a hoarse whisper; no one heard him or paid him any attention: they were too intent upon their pillage. He had forgotten to put on his scarlet cloak, and walked among them in the simple habit of a monk.

They jostled him aside; several times he was delivered a stinging blow to the face by some surly ruffian who identified him as an enemy. Other times he was simply jostled by an elbow, or received a solid kick in the shins. At first he scarcely seemed to give these blows any attention, but in time they accumulated and added to the already unbearable anguish he was carrying. He gave up his attempts to reach the mob and stood swaying uncertainly on his feet, his eyes glazed over with shock. Then round and round he was swept by the seething tide of human rabble, like a straw caught up in a whirlpool, buffeted first this way and then that, unable to defend himself or even cry out for help.

The last finely-strung wires of his mind suddenly snapped. And for a while he stood quite still while the crowd thinned out around him. He began to weep: a dry, discordant sound that only he could hear. One part of his disintegrated mind totted up his enormous debt to God. Then something strange transpired. He ceased to *care*. He even smiled, a curious, twisted parody of a smile. And slowly his mirth spread from around the corners of his mouth until his wrinkled face broke into a broad and idiotic grin.

He raised his arms and held them outstretched, like a bird. He took a dainty step forward, then swooped, describing an awkward circle in the small space around him. Then he crouched on his haunches and, arms flapping, began to crow like a cock. Seconds later he was standing upright again, a wild look in his eyes. He began to dance with a weird, shuffling movement such as a savage might make. A look of rapture and delight spread across his face and he danced faster, whirling round and round, seemingly unable to stop himself from spinning. A few mouths gaped in surprise at this crazy exhibition, and for a while the angry bustle of the crowd was stilled as they watched the antics of the Abbot.

Lost in the wild delirium of his whirling dance, he imagined them looking upon his performance with awe and reverence. Gradually he slowed down his wild spinning and flashed them an idiotic smile.

"Why, it's the old Abbot 'imself," someone commented. "He's gone clear off his rocker!"

Almost as swiftly as he had begun his wild dance, the Abbot brought it to a halt. He faced them with solemn dignity for a moment, then turned about so that he faced the scabrous 'miracle' that rose high above the valley, wafting its fetid stench towards them.

I recognize You now, he thought. For now he was convinced the Wall was indeed the work of the Adversary. God had not seen fit to punish him at all: it was the Devil who had sought to make him betray his trust in the Lord. Well, the Abbot knew well enough how to pay his respects to him. . .

He gave a graceful, mocking bow in the direction of The Wall. Then he turned around, bent over, pulled up his cassock and bared his backside to the Adversary. He waved his wrinkled old flesh from side to side, giggling happily to himself. He farted twice and fell over.

"The Abbot has lost his mind!" someone cried. "Look at him!" Did you see how he bared his bum and pranced around like a fool?''

"Aye," said another, surlier voice. "We well know the corruption of his nature and of this monastery. I say, to hell with them all!''

And for a beginning they closed in upon the sprawled figure of the Abbot with moblike, manufactured courage. They kicked and beat him until he was unconscious, and when they were weary of their ugly work they drifted off and resumed their search for food and drink. The Abbot was left twitching in the dust.

After a while he revived. His old face was a ruin where their fists had struck time and time again, his eyes so closed up that he could barely see. But slowly his addled wits came together and he began to crawl, crooning softly to himself the melody of some ancient psalm.

People continued to pour into the monastery seeking refuge from the valley. None of them gave any attention to the poor, battered creature crawling among them. The Abbot moved with the single-minded purpose of a doomed animal, conscious only of the desperate need to reach the sanctuary of his lodge.

Somehow he made it. Many times he was sent sprawling by hurrying feet, and once he was almost run down by a tumbril. But finally he reached the steps of his lodge and crawled inside. He closed the door and leaned against it, his legs spread out on the bare stone floor. He looked down at his bleeding hands, then at the steep flight of steps leading up to his eyrie.

I must try, he thought. *Once I am up there I will be safe. No one would try to break through that stout wooden door. . .*

The number of steps leading up through the tower seemed impossibly large, yet he knew he had to attempt them.

His hands and knees were raw. He sobbed, knowing what lay ahead of him before he found sanctuary. He ground his teeth together with manic determination. He crawled on

157

bleeding hands and knees towards the base of the steps.

Outside, the angry roar of the mob did not diminish.

●   ●   ●

When Conrad and Donella reached the southern flank of The Wall the view was astonishing. The Wall reached out several hundred yards beyond the rim of the valley, the once fine mist sullied with dark, foul-smelling droplets of water. Edge-on, the phenomenon showed no perceptible curvature; it was only that portion of it that covered almost half the valley that bulged outward so obscenely, its surface riddled with the dark, fetid fissures oozing their foul substance into the lake. The student could also discern a haze hanging over the water, in front of The Wall, like a fine mist. And from somewhere far off he imagined he could hear a high-pitched hissing sound that reminded him of steam escaping from a boiling kettle.

Even with the heavy masks which the girl had fashioned to tie around the bottom half of their faces, the foul odour was still overwhelming. The farther they had climbed up the slope, the more it had decreased in strength, but even here it was still strong enough to turn their stomachs. Conrad was determined to ignore it, lest it destroy his last opportunity to make a close observation of The Wall, and he encouraged Donella to do likewise. And so she did, sitting mute on horse-back while he made his calculations and entered them into his book of Records, her face white above the mask, her dark eyes expressionless.

The masks also made conversation difficult between them. But by now their understanding was so mutual that various inclinations of the head sufficed for Conrad to let her know what he was about, and when she should follow or remain still. She bore all this with patience.

All around them the air seemed charged with an ominous tension, as though every atom of its was being subjected to an intolerable strain.

158

For a moment Conrad put his observations aside and rode over to where the girl waited. He leaned his face close to hers, so that he would be heard through the cloth covering his lips. "I like not this sense of foreboding," he said. "Do you feel it?"

For answer she gave a nod. And clutched at his arm, holding it for a moment while he read the fear in her eyes.

Conrad frowned. "There is one more thing I would do: approach the lake as closely as possible to see those fissures clearly. . ."

Her eyes were wide and frightened.

"You need not come with me," he said gently. "I will work swiftly, for I fear that even with this cloth about my face, I will not be able to spend too long in front of that foul Wall. And see, Donella: the valley is almost deserted. Everyone is leaving. There is no one to trouble us."

This was so. Everyone was packing up and leaving the valley. Some had not even bothered to take their belongings with them; the ground where they had encamped was littered with all kinds of debris. It was a sorry sight. The path leading out of the valley was crowded with pilgrims and sightseers anxious to get away from the stench.

"Conrad," she said. "I will come with you. I have come this far."

He marked her proud, determined chin and did not challenge her decision to remain at his side. Nor would he have wanted to: this was no common girl but someone to walk beside for the rest of his life.

"Then we had best get moving," he said.

Having slept in so late, they now found that the sun was almost at its meridian: nearly half the day was gone. Turning their mounts, they made their way carefully back into the valley.

Behind them, Conrad's last marker stood more than a hundred yards from the far-flung edge of The Wall.

They reached the shore of the swollen, foul-smelling lake.

159

It rolled towards them like a dark tide of filth. It was only by a great effort of will and the determination of his rigorous training as a Scientist that Conrad was able to approach the very edge of this malodorous swamp; it could no longer be called a body of water. Donella followed, as though connected to him by some powerful, unseen force. Her shoulders drooped, but she made a conscious effort to duplicate the boy's movements.

From this vantage point, the face of The Wall was truly ghastly. It reminded Conrad of the scummy surface of a winter pond frozen over, and just beginning to crack and thaw, letting the slimy water bubble to the surface.

The fissures were enormous: some were many yards wide. And from them the great tides of dark ooze poured down into the 'lake'. The foul smell made the boy's head reel; he knew that he could not stay much longer at this spot. And yet. . . there were others less protected than themselves up to their waists in this tide of filth.

Only a short distance away a handful of monks still struggled to remove the last valuable remnants from their wooden dais. The main object of their endeavours was the heavy and cumbersome carving of the Child on the Wheel. Even as Conrad watched, he saw two of the worthy brothers slip on the platform, and the priceless carving tumbled into the lake. A groan went up from the monks. How could they hope to salvage it now?

The sun had dipped a few degrees behind The Wall. A new and even more ugly countenance now glared down at them. And the high-pitched hissing sound seemed even more pronounced than before.

The heavens groaned again. The sound was so shattering that they pressed their hands over their ears. The ground shuddered. Their horses neighed and pranced around. Suddenly the dark lake surged towards them in one mighty wave and lashed at the feet of their mounts. They had to grapple with their reins to calm the animals down, and turn them to higher ground. All around the heavens shook and thundered and echoed as though the sky itself was about to burst.

Trapped in the foul swamp of the lake, the monks looked up in fear at the terrible changes now taking place in The Wall. It bulged suddenly forward. The great fissures widened and soon great runnels of the dark ooze were pouring down, accompanied by great gouts of water.

Conrad tore the cloth from his face. "Donella—go back!" he cried, waving with his free hand. Together they cantered a good distance from the shore.

Again the heavens groaned and the earth shook and they had to struggle to control their mounts. Thunder hammered at their eardrums; the pressure became almost unbearable.

Pressure. . .

A light dawned suddenly in the boy's eyes. *Of course!* Why had it taken him so long to fit together the pieces of the puzzle? The outward curvature of The Wall constantly increasing. The high-pitched hiss and the fine mist hanging over the lake, such as he had seen rising from the base of a waterfall. The sudden enlarging of the fissures and the groaning of the sky, as if The Wall were holding back some intolerable *pressure.* In which case. . .

"Ride, Donella!" he cried, making his voice heard even above the thunder that reverberated all around them. "Stay close by me—but ride for your life! We must get out of this valley!"

She did not pause to question his command. Her heels dug into the flanks of her mare. They galloped across the uneven ground, Conrad leading.

The path out of the valley was crowded with people. "Go around them!" he urged. "Watch the ground! Be careful lest you be thrown!"

They rode in a wide arc that took them around the path and up a steeper incline. Behind them the heavens groaned even louder, as though ready to give up their terrible secret.

The monks had abandoned their attempt to salvage their wooden Child and were struggling through the fetid swamp towards the shore. Their eyes were filled with fear; perhaps by now they guessed what had impelled the boy and girl to gallop for safety.

They almost made it. But then there came a sound like a thousand thunderclaps; an unseen force knocked people to the ground and toppled Conrad and Donella from their horses when they were only a few yards from the rim of the valley.

The boy rolled a short distance. Dazed, he first looked *up*—and not around. And he saw from end to mighty end The Wall break open, unleashing a mighty torrent of mud and water into the valley.

The wretched monks never stood a chance. Within seconds this enormous cataract swept out to submerge the valley floor and great waves reached up the slopes. People still on the pathway screamed and struggled to reach the top of the valley before the surging tide sucked them back. It was a hideous spectacle. Their screams could not even be heard above the thunder of those gigantic waves.

Conrad felt a tug at his wrist. For him fate had been fortunate: he had fallen with his reins still looped around his hand and his mount was tugging nervously at them. Of Donella's horse there was no sign: it had obviously galloped off in fright. The girl was lying half-conscious only a short distance away. He crawled towards her.

"Donella!" he cried, his lips almost touching her ear. "Get up—quickly!"

She struggled to her feet, half-listening to his words, half-watching the terrible sight in the valley. The boy mounted his horse and helped her up so that she sat behind him. And this time her hands went around him and grasped him so tight that he gasped for breath. Then he swung away from the scene and sent his mount scrambling over the rim of the valley and out into the open.

162

Behind him the mighty cataract continued to pour down. But he never once looked back. He knew only too well the nature of the doom pursuing them; he rode like a man possessed.

Once clear of the valley their destination was predictable. All around them the land was as flat as a tablecloth, except for one small rise.

To the monastery Conrad rode, as though all the devils in hell were snapping at his heels.

TWELVE

The sundering flood

The roar of the raging cataract was now the only sound in all the world. It drowned the hysterical cries of the people flee-ing from the valley and made conversation impossible among the gaping crowd which had paused on the road lead-ing back to Northbridge. Because they were so far beyond the valley they assumed they were secure. Conrad knew better, and this explained his feverish haste.

He had no way of knowing how fast the valley was filling, but he guessed that already the waters had surged more than halfway up the slopes, sweeping aside a vast number of people from their path and sucking them down to their death. The monks would have died almost instantly, he realized. And poor Mallory—what of him? Ah, it was useless to bemoan the fate of a few when so many would die.

He rode clear of the road, cutting diagonally across the open ground to reach the monastery in the shortest possible time. Behind him the mighty cataract still thundered down from the sky, with no sign of abating.

Hundreds of people had gathered together outside the monastery walls, gazing with awe upon the cataclysm that had split The Wall asunder and let loose the great waterfall. At this stage they had no notion of the fate that would soon overtake them, and Conrad wasted no time in trying to tell them: the safety of the girl and himself was now his only motivation.

He dismounted quickly, helping Donella down. The crowd was too fascinated by the distant cataract to pay them any

164

attention, and this worked to their advantage. He pushed a way through the throng and they were soon inside the walls.

The monastery was almost deserted. "Quickly," he said, holding fast to her hand. "The Abbot's lodge. . ."

They ran as fast as they could across the open ground. And only now did Donella begin to grasp the terrible urgency that spurred the boy on. She gasped and looked up at the tower rising high above the Abbot's private dwelling. It was by far the highest point to be found anywhere inside the monastery.

The door pushed open easily; it was not even locked. When they were safe inside Conrad bolted it securely, shaking his head when he saw that the wood had grown rotten with age.

"Up the stairs!" he shouted. It was the only way to make himself heard above the roar of the distant cataract.

He pushed her ahead of him up the steep steps. She came to a sudden halt at the top of the stairs. He was about to ask her what was the matter when he saw the reason for her stopping: there was a body sprawled across the open doorway. He pushed her gently to one side and stepped forward.

He looked down at the bruised and battered face of the Abbot. "Good God!" he cried. "What have the fools done to him?"

A cursory examination revealed that the old man was still alive, but unconscious. When the boy saw his raw and bleeding hands he wondered how he had managed to climb the stairs at all.

He stepped over the body and into the Abbot's private study. Then he stooped and grasped the old man's arms and dragged him across the threshold. There was a bed in one corner. He rolled the Abbot on to his back and slid his arms underneath the old man's shoulders. He looked imploringly at Donella. "Give me a hand!" he cried. The girl came forward, and, with her hefting the Abbot's frail legs, they managed to manoeuvere his unconscious body into a comfortable position on the ornate bed. This done, the boy turned his attention to more urgent matters.

There were three stout bolts on the door; he threw them home woth savage satisfaction. He thumped on the heavy, six-inch thick slab of wood and was satisfied; with any luck it would hold. Then he looked quickly around, searching for suitable furniture. He grasped a heavy oak chest and began dragging it towards the door. Donella guessed what he was about and lent her own considerable strength to the effort.

They rammed it hard up against the door, then piled other furniture around and above it: brocaded chairs, a large and beautifully carved table and three smaller ones; two large cabinets. The girl never stopped pushing and heaving long enough to ask Conrad why he made these preparations; the continuing roar of the cataract was sufficient explanation. For by now even her untrained mind had begun to glean some idea of what was about to happen.

Scarcely had they completed their preparations to the boy's satisfaction than a great roar went up from below; it was even audible above the thunder of the raging waters.

Conrad's expression was grim. "Donella!" he called out. "Stay away from the window! I don't want anyone to see us, to have any idea we are here!"

She nodded. But her face was white. Even standing where she was, she had glimpsed something through the window; she knew the reason why the crowd below had succumbed to panic.

"Conrad!" she called out, gesturing for him to join her. He did so, knowing in advance what he would see from her vantage point: for already a different thunder had joined the roar of the cataract, but this time it came from the *ground*: a great swelling sound that shook the walls of the tower.

It was just as he had feared. The valley had become a vast lake. The mighty waterfall showed no sign of diminishing; the only change he could detect was in the nature of the sound it made now that it poured down into a deep lake.

The lake had overflowed. Water poured away in every direction. And a great wave, nearly forty feet high, was racing towards the monastery. It was this terrible sight which had caused the people below to bellow in fright, and the ground beneath their feet to tremble.

The advancing wave swept everything before it: tumbrils, horses, screaming people—all were devoured by the advancing wall of water. In seconds it would reach the monastery. . .

The crowd were driven into a frenzy. Without looking down, Conrad knew they would be running inside, running for their lives, searching for some high point where they might be safe from the great wave. Some would be scaling walls while others scurried up staircases; it would be pandemonium, and only he guessed rightly that their efforts would be to no avail.

The sides of the Abbot's tower rose sheer and smooth; it could not be climbed. The only way into their room was by the staircase. If they were lucky, no one would reach it in time. If they were not. . . then he was prepared to defend their sanctuary with his life.

There was still time for him to take Donella in his arms and tell her that all would be well; she was shivering and cold, like a frightened bird. Then he heard the hammering of many feet pounding up the stairs outside the door.

"Quick!" he cried, and hurried over to lean his weight against the pile of furniture. The girl did not hesitate but took up her position beside him, leaning hard against the oak press. For a moment their eyes locked; the spectre of death seemed to hang between them.

There came a sudden pounding on the heavy wooden door, a sound even more terrifying than the thunder of the advancing wall of water.

"Who's in there?" cried a voice. "Let us in! Let us in, or we will drown! *Let us in!*"

Conrad remained silent and grim-lipped. The door moved

slightly as the combined weight of several hefty shoulders rammed against it—but the bolts and hinges held. The Abbot's mason had built well when he had constructed the tower.

Conrad began to sweat. But his sweat was cold, like ice on his flesh. "We must not let them in!" he cried, above the approaching roar and the pervading thunder. "If we do they will kill us!"

Again the door shook. Again the feeble cries were heard. The boy reached for his sword, praying that the door would hold, that he would not have to use his weapon. He leaned close to the girl. "Donella, if they break in. . . if I die. . !"

He did not need to explain any further. "I have my knife," she answered, and held it ready in her right hand.

The cries outside gave way to curses, then to whining and crying; but the boy's heart held fast. He knew that these men must die.

If we can only hold out a moment or two longer, he kept thinking.

Suddenly the pounding on the door grew more desperate than before. There were shrieks and screams and then the tower shook as though a giant fist had struck it. Conrad shut his eyes, trying to blot out the picture of the gigantic wall of water crashing down on the monastery, sweeping everything in its path.

Would the walls hold? Would their building stand fast against such a blow? Would the foundations survive such an onslaught?

They would soon know.

The screams on the other side of the door rose to a pitch and then faded away into gasps and struggling cries as the momentum of the water swept in through the door of the lodge and surged up the staircase. The people outside were swept and tossed around like so much straw, then sucked down to the bottom of the stairs.

Water began to spread through the room, forcing its way

168

underneath the door. In seconds they were ankle-deep in the dark, foul-smelling liquid.

"Conrad!" The girl cried out, and clung to him. There was little more he could do than return her embrace. For it seemed now that they would surely die, along with everyone else.

Another great fist shook the tower. And another. Yet still it stood firm and resolute above the raging waters. Then gradually the level of the water began to fall in their room; soon only a scummy surface slime remained.

The boy could hardly believe their good fortune. He rushed to the window and looked out. He was hoping to see at least a handful of survivors clinging to other rooftops, but such was not the case.

A great torrent of water rushed by barely ten feet below their window. There was not another rooftop projecting above the flood: their tower had become a solitary island in a vast inland sea. There was nothing but water for as far as his eyes could see. And to the north, where once the magnificent, mysterious Wall had been suspended, there was still a mighty cataract pouring down from the sky, unchecked.

"Dear God," he whispered, "how much longer can this go on?" He thought of the towns and the cities that lay in the path of this great flood. Northbridge. . . *Abingdon*. And Asquith riding back as fast as he could, with no idea of the terrible fate that awaited him!

The boy sat down in one of the Abbot's ornate chairs and buried his face in his hands. The concept was too vast for him to grasp. Oh, the tragedy of it!

Donella came over quietly and placed one hand upon his bowed head. She leaned her face close to his, and said: "I know. I know how you must feel. All those people. . . gone. And for no reason."

He looked up. *"Reason?* Dear girl, you cannot expect nature to be reasonable: that is the province of mankind, though poorly practised. But, Donella, I have been thinking

169

even further ahead—of the thousands of people who have yet to die before that sweeping flood. . .''

She looked out the window and saw what he had seen. They seemed to be all alone in the middle of a great ocean. And suddenly she was gripped by a new fear. She swung around, facing him. "How long do you think the flood will last?"

He shook his head. "I have no way of even guessing, not while yonder cataract continues to fall. Let us pray our Abbot has enough food and drink stored up here to see us through."

His mention of the old man brought his presence back into the room. "Oh," she said, "I had forgotten him."

She hurried over to his bed. The Abbot was still lying on the bed as they had left him; but now his eyes were open; he had regained consciousness. He gave her a weak, uncomprehending smile. And when she looked down on his tragic face she was moved to do something to help him.

A quick search of his well-appointed study revealed, among other valuable items, a wash-basin and a large pitcher filled with fresh water. Some face-cloths and towels were placed nearby.

"Go easy with the water!" Conrad called out, watching her. "We will need every drop."

Donella dipped only the corner of a cloth into the pitcher, and used this to bathe the old man's face. With another corner she moistened his cracked lips. They managed to form the words 'thank you', but no sound was forthcoming. The Abbot was grateful for the cool cloth she lay upon his burning flesh.

Conrad drew the Abbot's largest chair close to the window and stayed there for the remainder of the day. At sunset some details became apparent that had not been visible before: on either side of the distant cataract were cracked remnants of the original Wall. From the fissures smaller rivulets ran down to feed the growing flood; the dying sun

170

helped to spread a cancerous light over the inland sea.

Dusk drew a welcome veil over this unpleasant sight. Donella found some candles and lit two; one she placed at the Abbot's bedside, the other she brought close to the window and set it down on one of the small tables.

She had left Conrad alone with his thoughts for many hours; she knew full well the terrible burden he must bear. But now she came close and stood beside him, her hand on his arm. Together they looked out into the encroaching night. A weird phosphorescent light seemed to weave around the great waterfall, coming and going with an irregular rhythm. The boy thought it very strange, but no stranger than anything else he had witnessed.

She said clearly: "The Abbot keeps a good larder: we shall not want for food. He has bread and wine, cheese and sausage, and a great variety of pickled vegetables and other things. But only that one pitcher of water."

This news brought some relief to the student: they would not starve for many a day.

Donella prepared a simple supper. She even managed to help the Abbot into a sitting position and plied him with a few sips of port. This seemed to help the old man considerably; he thanked her with several nods and afterwards she managed to get him to eat a small slice of bread, washed down with a little water. "My share," she said, smiling at the boy. Conrad said nothing.

The Abbot was soon fast asleep and breathing steadily.

"There is room enough on his bed for another, Conrad," she said. "You look so weary."

He shook his head. He was by now too firmly established by the window to want to move. "This chair will do; it is comfortable enough. But you might fetch me a blanket; the night carries an uncommon chill." Perhaps it had been brought about by the presence of so much water surrounding them.

She brought him the blanket, but instead of handing it to

171

him she stood facing him for a moment, her back to the open window. And at long last her face crumpled; the effort of keeping up a bold front for so long finally failed her. "Oh, Conrad," she sighed. Her eyes filled with tears.

He held out his arms and she collapsed against him, whimpering. And there she remained for the rest of the night. The Abbot's chair was large and elaborate enough to hold their two bodies, pressed close together to ward off the cold. One blanket was sufficient.

She soon ceased crying. He raised her chin with one hand and placed his lips timidly upon her moist lids. A tiny tremor passed through her. Then she took his hand and placed it softly over her left breast. She kept it there until she fell asleep. He was reluctant to withdraw it; the presence of her soft, warm breast under his palm was tenderly reassuring. He had no way of knowing what their fate might be, but now, for this moment, they at least had each other.

Shortly before Conrad fell asleep, the moon rose and shed its light across the inland sea. It picked out the incongruous image of the weathercock that he remembered seeing on the abbey roof.

"The level of the water is dropping," he said. But the sleeping girl did not hear him. Well, no sense in disturbing her; his news could wait.

And so at last he drifted off, with new-found hope to ease his sleep.

•　　•　　•

By morning most of the roofs of the highest monastery buildings had reappeared above the flood. The distant cataract no longer boomed and thundered; it had settled down to a steady, even flow.

But they had to wait another two days and nights before the water had receded enough for them to come down from their high sanctuary and set foot on the mud-choked grounds of the monastery.

The Abbot had recovered with surprising speed, but except for his occasional nods and lop-sided grins, he maintained a curious silence. Only once had he spoken, and his words had not seemed to be directed at either one of them, but to the world in general.

"The Lord has seen fit to visit a second Flood upon us," he croaked, staring wild-eyed from the window. "In this way will our sins be washed away."

He accompanied them on their outside expedition. "I think his mind is nearly gone," Conrad whispered to the girl.

The walls surrounding the monastery had been reduced to rubble by the force of the flood. Beyond them, the remainder of the land was still under water. Inside, great waves of silt had piled up against the buildings, all of which were still standing in mute testimony to the skill of their masons. And embedded among these great heaps of mud were dead bodies and other debris. Already the tireless sun had begun to bake these monuments into a collage of death.

They tramped through the heavy mud and explored some of the other buildings, hoping to find something useful. Everywhere the cellars had become deep, watery graves, soon it became obvious their search was futile.

They returned to the tower, the Abbot muttering something vague under his breath. Donella checked their meagre supplies. They had hardly touched the water, preferring to ease their thirst with the Abbot's wine, one small sip at a time.

The boy stared out of the window; Donella stood beside him, searching for his thoughts. "I do not know how long it will be before we can leave the monastery," he said quietly. And even then, he did not think much of their chances. "We had best ration our food carefully." The nearest town was Northbridge, and they would have to make their way through deep mud to get there. Not that he expected to find much left standing: the rampaging flood would have swept most of the old houses away as though they were made of

173

paper. But he could not give up hope entirely.

"Tomorrow," he murmured. "Tomorrow the situation should have improved. . ."

"I have been thinking," the girl said. "We might have to stay here for some time before anyone comes to rescue us. Do you think they will send anyone, Conrad?"

He shook his head. "I cannot say. We have no way of knowing how widespread this disaster has been. People many miles away may have more than enough to cope with without worrying about possible survivors here. If this be the case, then we must be prepared to make our own way to the coast, on foot, across miles of mudflats."

She looked him straight in the eye, head high. "I also have considered that, Conrad. And I am ready." Her left hand clasped his. A strange, wistful look appeared in her eyes and she leaned against him. "Tell me again about Abingdon." Since they had arrived at their sanctuary she had never once mentioned her father, or Hakim; but several times she had asked him about Abingdon: sweet Abingdon which by now might be no more. . .

Conrad did not suggest this to Donella. Instead, he spoke, as he had often done before during the long nights of their ordeal, of the College and his friends; of the gentle river and the splendid gardens. "It is indeed a beautiful place," he said, his throat suddenly dry and aching.

"And will I really be able to wear dresses. . . and perhaps jewellery? And let my hair grow?"

"Of course." It did not harm to encourage Donella in her desire to know more about his world; it was positively helpful if it urged her to believe that there really was another world beyond *this*.

●　　●　　●

That night the Abbot came and stood by the window for a long time, while the candles burned low. He seemed fascinated by the strange, phosphorescent glow that glimmered and

174

danced and sometimes disappeared altogether, in the place where the water flowed down from the sky.

Conrad, seated in his comfortable chair to the Abbot's left, heard the old man mutter, "He is waiting for me . . . out there. Waiting to punish me. . . for my sins. Can you not see His Divine light summoning me? Yea, I will take on to my own shoulders all our sins, just as His only Child took upon Himself the sins of our forefathers. . ."

Donella, who had arranged a chair of her own to be near Conrad, took the old man gently by the arm and led him back to his bed. He made no effort to resist, but went with her as meekly as a lamb.

As she drew the coverlet over him he spoke to her in a voice that was little more than a croaking whisper. "God is waiting for me. . . out there. Can you not see Him?"

The girl made soothing sounds and gently shushed him, but the Abbot would not close his eyes. He rolled over on to his left side so that he could still look out of the window at the weird glow in the sky.

Conrad sat motionless in his chair, his eyes staring fixedly at the same strange light that fascinated the Abbot, but seeing in it something else.

Donella came over to him. "What ails thee, Conrad?" she said, stroking his cheek. And suddenly he clutched at her hand as a drowning man might grasp at anything to keep him afloat.

He replied in a flat voice, without looking up: "I fear for our future, Donella."

"But the waters will go down. . . eventually." She drew his head forward until it rested against her breast, and stroked his tangled blond hair as though comforting a child afraid of the dark. "You need rest, my darling. You told me yourself that all would be well."

He turned his face to one side, feeling her warm breast against his cheek. "But *will* it? I cannot be sure! Oft I have felt inclined to agree with those who would have it that our

175

world is but a madman's dream. . ."

"You cannot say such a thing!" She could feel his bitterness surging through him like a vicious bile and was helpless against it.

"No?" He looked up, drew himself away and slumped back in his chair. In the flickering sandelight he looked suddenly much older. . . and very weary. "But you see, Donella, I have lost my faith. Not for the first time; I was once a novice, long ago it seems now, in such a monastery at this. Do you find that hard to believe?"

She shook her head, puzzled by this abrupt change in his manner. "No," she answered truthfully. "To me you have always seemed. . . devout."

"Devout? How strange that you should use that word! Yes, for a while I was. First, when I was only a child within the Church—scarcely nine years old! But when I grew older and began asking questions, important questions to which I was given no answer, I found I could no longer believe in the teachings of the Church. I lost my faith—but only for a while. For then I turned to Science; it at least provided some answers to this fantastic world we live in. And I revelled in an atmosphere of freedom of the mind such as I had not known as a novice. But having given my faith to another, Donella, I fear that she, too, has proved a strumpet. Science cannot help us now. . ."

She bowed her head. It was not in her to chide him. But from some deep resource of which she herself had been unaware, she found the courage to say: "Perhaps it is not necessary to have faith in any specific thing, merely to know that somewhere there is *something* worth having faith in."

He gave her a strange look.

She kissed him goodnight and blew out the candles. The Abbot snored softly, his troubled mind at last given over to sleep. Conrad and Donella sat in their separate chairs, a few paces apart, with a blanket each. And without another word they soon drifted off.

176

Sometime later, Conrad was roused by the *absence* of a familiar sound. At first he thought something had affected his hearing—but he could clearly hear Donella's steady breathing.

He threw aside his blanket and went over to the window. In the distance the strange phosporescent glow still lingered, but there was no sign of the waterfall.

The cataract had ceased!

Excited, he turned to the girl and shook her shoulder gently. "Donella, the waterfall—it's stopped! Do you hear me? Stopped at last!"

The moonlight shone full upon her upturned face. Her dazed, sleepy look soon changed to one of joy. "Oh, Conrad!"

"Come—see for yourself." He took her hand and led her to the window.

They both looked out in wonder at the peaceful waters. The girl leaned against him, breathing a heartfelt sigh of relief. "Then everything will be all right, just as you said."

He held her tight. "Of course it will. Wait and see."

● ● ●

It was Donella who shook him roughly awake next morning. "Conrad—please wake. Quickly!" There was a sharp edge of urgency in her voice.

He was instantly awake and alert. He saw her worried face looking down at him. "What is it?" he asked. "What's the matter?"

"It's the Abbot. He's wandered off."

"What? Ah, the old fool! Wandered where?"

She pointed towards the window. "He's out there, amongst all that mud and filth. He seems to be trying to reach the lake, where the valley used to be."

Conrad leapt to the window and looked out. Sure enough, far in the distance he spied a solitary, tiny figure weaving its way through the great dunes of mud thrown up by the flood.

Even as he watched, the figure disappeared behind one of these and was lost from sight.

"He muttered something about going to meet the Lord," Donella said. "Don't you remember?"

The boy nodded, his face creased into a worried frown. What should he do—let the old fool look after himself, perhaps even drown himself? No, that was out of the question: too many had died already. Besides, the Abbot was their only witness to all that had happened, even though his wits were a little askew.

"I'll go after him and bring him back."

Donella was relieved by his decision. "Be careful," She implored. "If that dreadful waterfall should return. . ."

"I think not, my lady: that cataract has been well spent." He felt it necessary to reassure her, even though he had no way of knowing whether or not the flood would return.

He hurried towards the door. 'The old fool has quite a start on me," he said, "but I should be able to catch him up before he reaches the lake."

She put her arms around him and kissed him with the same deep fervour he remembered.

He stroked her hair. "I shall not be long. Keep watch for me by the window."

And then he was gone, hurrying down the steep staircase and out into the mud-filled monastery grounds.

Donella watched him leave, saw him pass through the great gap in the rubble that had once been the high monastery walls, and set off across the sea of mud. He turned around once and waved, then moved off after the old man.

She stood with her hands clasped tight together, her lips forming the words of an unspoken benediction. Waiting.

THIRTEEN

The fortress at the end of time

For a great distance around the deep lake the flood had piled up great mountains of mud and silt. A cloudless sky and an industrious sun was slowly sculpturing these into solid mounds. Scattered between them were pools of brackish salt water of every shape and size; some miniature lakes, others no more than puddles to be stepped over.

Conrad found the going difficult, and marvelled at the Abbot's pace. He found the business of keeping his footing a constant worry, yet this did not seem to be a problem to the old man, driven on as he was by a divine vision he had fashioned for himself.

The sky was absolutely clear above the lake. Except for a puzzling shimmer that hung over it—rather like a heat-haze on a summer's day—there was no sign to indicate that anything out of the ordinary had occurred here. Yet the valley was gone, and had taken many lives with it.

Conrad was constantly reminded of this appalling loss of life as he trudged his way around the dunes, dodging the wide stretches of water where the sun winked back. From these mountains of silt projected, from time to time, arms and legs and dead faces leering out at him, along with all kinds of debris. Once he saw the carcass of a horse and, farther on, sunlight glanced off swords and lances. The remains of fine clothing, discoloured and encrusted with mud, were entangled with coarse peasant cloth.

What a strange monument this will make, he thought. That is, if it were allowed to stand. Perhaps the proper and

179

human thing to do would be to remove all the dead and give them a decent burial. But that would take time. . . and many willing hands. Meanwhile the dead would decay at their leisurely pace.

He pressed on after the Abbot.

Suddenly he was brought to an abrupt halt by the sight of an unexpected object embedded in a dune. Most of it was visible, only a portion of it being buried in the mud. It was the wooden carving of the Child on the Wheel which the monks had struggled so valiantly to salvage. Never before had the agony of His expression seemed so fitting. The boy felt a sharp pang in his chest—a pain reflected in the seven arrows, most of which were now only broken shafts, buried in the Saviour's breast. For a moment his mind was filled with an adoration from his childhood. But the feeling soon passed and he hurried on after the Abbot. Behind him the carven idol continued to stare sightlessly at the toiling sun.

It was some time later that Conrad realized he was lost. He found himself without a reference point: the mountains of mud hid both the monastery and the lake from view. He was desperately afraid that he might be trudging around in circles and that he would never catch up with the old man.

"Hallo!" he called out, hoping to attract the Abbot's attention. He repeated the call three times, but received no answer. Even if he had been heard, there was no guarantee the Abbot would answer, so intent had he become upon his purpose.

Exasperated and angry at letting himself get into such a situation, the boy plunged forward recklessly weaving in and out among the dunes, anxiously looking for something he could recognize. He tried to remember how the landscape had looked from the window of the Abbot's study: close by the lake the land was relatively smooth. . . the rolling dunes of mud only began some distance from its shore. Well, that was something to look for. . .

He ploughed on through the mud. Occasionally strange

creatures flopped about in some of the deeper puddles. Once he stooped to examine one: it was identical with the creature he had seen in Asquith's flask, only this specimen was nearly a foot long, and its human attributes were even more impressive. It stared back at the student with the same indefinable expression.

The boy shuddered. This creature, and many more like it, had obviously been brought here by the cataract. . . and somehow survived. But the fact that any creature could live in water and look so much like a vestigal human being terrified him. He hurried on.

Later he heard a strange humming. He increased his pace; when he rounded the next dune, sure enough, there was the figure of the Abbot striding determinedly away from him, musing aloud to himself to the tune of an ancient chant.

Conrad was about to call out and rush up to greet the old man. . . but something held him back. Perhaps it was curiosity: they were clear of the mud dunes and the shore of the lake was in sight. And he was puzzled by that strange shimmer hovering above it.

He turned around. There lay the monastery, sharp and clear in the distance. He breathed easily again. He would let the Abbot complete his pilgrimage, make sure that he came to no harm by throwing himself in the lake in a fit of religious zeal, then they would return to the monastery. . . and to Donella.

The frail figure of the Abbot trudged on, head down, hands clasped across his chest. The boy followed, maintaining a discreet distance between them. He did not wish to interfere with an old man's final pilgrimage.

The Abbot seemed to have no set point in mind; he chose to proceed in this fashion until he found a site that suited him. He kept a distance of at least a hundred yards between himself and the lake, which fact made Conrad feel a lot easier. He only hoped the old man would not take too long making up his mind where to stop and make peace with his

God.

It was difficult for the boy to work out the precise location where The Wall had been, but the position of the shimmering air seemed to provide a vital clue: could it be the final remnant of that disastrous 'miracle'? He marked its location carefully. Yes, it did seem to coincide with where The Wall had been. In another few moments they would be abreast of it and standing where the farthest flanks of the phenomenon had reached outside the valley.

He turned his attention away from this tantalizing shimmer in the sky and looked ahead.

The Abbot had disappeared.

The boy blinked. No more than a few yards had separated them, yet now there was no sign of the old man.

But that was impossible!

He looked quickly round. There was nowhere the Abbot could hide: the ground swept away for several hundred yards before the dunes began. Not even his agile old legs could have managed to cross such a distance in the space of a few short seconds. *Where,* then?

The boy stepped forward.

And gasped like a stranded fish. Daylight disappeared. The world around him changed with a terrifying suddenness. Gone were the lake and the mountains of silt, gone too the distant monastery. Instead he was surrounded by an eerie twilight. Overhead was a sky devoid of moon and stars. A deathly stillness pervaded the air.

He shook his head.

He took a step back.

A golden sun burned fiercely in the sky. All around him was the familiar ugliness of the flooded world. And before him: no sign of the Abbot.

He took a deep breath and stepped forward. And this time consciously passed through a faint shimmer in the air that was an extension of the haze hanging over the lake, but which he had not been aware of before.

182

Daylight disappeared. Again he stood surrounded by the same eerie twilight, gasping for breath. When he turned and looked behind him, there was no sign of the world he had left behind, only a featureless plain stretching into deep and utter darkness.

Realization broke over him like a wave: *I have crossed through into another world!* Galileo's theory was proven: the interface between *this* world had weakened sufficiently to allow a great flood to pass through, and even small creatures like himself and those strange half-humans flopping around in their little puddles on the *other* side of the interface.

But *how* and *why* had this weakness been brought about?

He spied a small figure some distance ahead: it was the Abbot toiling up a steep slope. Even in this dim-lit world his gait was unmistakable. Conrad hesitated, then set off after him.

The old man seemed to have become remarkably agile, ascending the smooth slope with astonishing speed. Yet after a while the boy discovered that his own progress was equally fast: and he had the uneasy sensation that each step seemed to take him just that little bit forward in *time* as well as *space*. It was all very confusing. One half of him cried out to go back, to retreat from this world into the relative safety of his own, before he was unable to do so. But his Scientific curiosity drove him on, even there.

Try as he would, Conrad could not gain ground on the Abbot. And although the air was still and devoid of any noise, it carried an oppressive tension.

The Abbot reached the top of the slope and disappeared over it. As Conrad struggled after him, he heard the far-off sound of surf; the first sound to intrude upon this darkened world.

His face itched. His body ached in every muscle. His eyes seemed to be on fire, so intense was the pain behind them. Yet he pressed on. He had to find out for himself what lay on the other side of this steep slope. . .

183

When he reached the top he froze. So too had the Abbot, only a few paces from him. They both looked out over an extraordinary world. Before them was the shore of a mighty ocean, strangely subdued, its waves breaking gently upon the shoals. To their left was an enormous crater, several miles wide. Conrad peered over the edge; even in the eerie twilight he could make out that its sides were slimy with mud and that a faint glimmer of murky water lay at the bottom. He did a quick mental calculation and realized that this was where the great flood had originated: the crater had once been a great lake, which had poured its contents into Conrad's world. But *how* had this been made possible?

The sea was the colour of jade in this land deprived of sunlight. To their right he could see that the land was broken up into a vast number of lakes both large and small, and similar lakes continued past the great crater on his left. This much at least was visible in the half-light.

For one terrifying moment he had a mental picture of him- self as some near-microscopic creature standing among a group of rock pools by the shore of an ocean in his own world. He shook his head in an effort to drive away the image, but it persisted. And he found that he lacked the courage to investigate any of the nearby lakes, for fear of what he would find: creatures half-fish, half-human, sport- ing close to the surface.

What kind of place is this? he wondered.

The Abbot gave a cry and stumbled forward. Conrad looked up and saw the reason for his sudden outburst.

A veil of fog seemed to have lifted from over the sea. And from the deep, jade-coloured water there rose a marvellous building. Its sides were smooth and sheer and its ramparts disappeared into the twilight. It was a thousand times more vast than any cathedral the boy had ever seen; for some reason he could not explain he thought of it as a fortress. For why else build it in the sea, so far from land?

Its walls were featureless; not a single projection marked

its smooth perfection. And it *glowed:* shifting patterns of white and golden lights whirled and danced within its substance. And what would that substance be? the student wondered. But he already suspected the answer: like nothing on earth.

The Abbot staggered a few paces farther, then fell to his knees on the alien shore, his hands clasped in prayer.

Conrad could not move. *Is this your God?* he asked silently of the old man. *If so, then I hope you are well pleased. But as for me. . . .*

He made an effort to join the old man. He had taken only two steps when he realized that an abrupt change had occured in this world. The twilight deepened into darkness; only the swirling lights inside the fortress and the reflections from the sea illuminated the landscape. And he recognized the source of the strange phosphorescent lights they had seen behind the waterfall at night: they came from this fantastic fortress.

The Abbot was muttering hysterically, yet the boy could scarcely see him in the weak illumination. Then the darkness began to contract, to form isolated whirlpools of even deeper blackness. The sky regained its former twilight, only a little brighter than before. The whirlpools of darkness drew tighter and tighter together; they formed an absolute blackness almost impossible to look at. And very slowly they advanced upon the fortress.

Lightning flashed across the sky. No, not lightning: these savage arcs of light were unlike anything the boy had ever seen, accompanying the swirling whirlpools of darkness as they approached the towering fortress rising from the sea.

In another moment, hell was unleashed.

The globes of darkness attacked like any intelligent, well-drilled regiment. They spread out into great coils and wrapped themselves like leeches against the bright walls of the fortress. Others rose with astonishing speed and attacked the topmost ramparts of the building, far out of sight.

185

The fortress retaliated. The gentle fires that had danced within its walls changed to vibrant, violet hues. Flashes of red and violet fire lashed out at the coils of darkness; and some of those dark whirlpools fell away from the walls, trailing a smoky greyness down into the sea. But others clung on tenaciously, gnawing away with their fierce energy at the defences of the fortress. And away in the distance, the boy could see fresh battalions of darkness gathering. The fortress was aware of this; even while it fought to dislodge the ugly spheres of darkness still clinging to its walls, it hurled out great lances of fire at these distant whirlpools of absolute blackness. Some of the lances struck home and turned the whirlpools into churning, drifting ashes. Others, misdirected, spent their energy in the ground.

Conrad almost lost his footing as the shock waves of these terrible explosions reached him. They certainly sent the old man sprawling—but not for long. He was soon crawling forward on his knees, as though the effort of standing was not worth while.

"My lord Abbot!" the student cried. It was time to be getting away from this place. He hurried forward, while all around him the air screamed and hammered, as ancient adversaries enjoined themselves once more to battle.

He realized now that they had *come through* into this world during a lull in an eternal conflict, and that they had best escape as quickly as they could. Nothing human could possibly live in this strange world of mysterious forces and enigmatic buildings that rose from the sea like monuments to the beginning of time.

Conrad's face itched. He reached up to scratch it. His hand froze, his fingers finding a dense growth of stubble on his cheeks. Stunned, he looked down at his hands: the veins stood out from his skin. They were the hands of a stranger. . .

The Abbot collapsed in the sand only a few paces ahead. Conrad staggered forward, and turned the old man over as

186

gently as he could. But the tortured, toothless face that stared back was not the man he remembered. The Abbot's hair was white. The old man seemed to have aged several decades, and even now the light was fading from his eyes. He raised one limp hand and waved the student away. His lips formed the words *'Go. . . back'*, and his weak hand repeated the gesture. Then his eyes glazed over and the boy knew that he was dead.

Dead.

He stood up, staring down at his strange hands. This was not only a battlefield; it was a battle*when*: time moved differently here, just as Galileo had postulated it might in other dimensions. And in this world it might even become a weapon. . .

It was no place for man. Or, if man had ever had a place in this world, he had deserted it long ago and reverted to the simple aquatic creature Conrad had first seen in the flask: he had devolved and left his empire to the strange forces and powers he had, perhaps, unleashed in his quest for knowledge.

Conrad had no idea how long this terrible battle had been waging between the devouring darkness and the shining fortress. Perhaps its beginnings were lost in the mists of time, and there might never be an end to the conflict. But one outcome was certain: the titanic warfare was weakening the fabric of space and time that separated the infinite number of words postulated by Galileo: not only Conrad's world, but others too must surely suffer.

And I have become a man, he realized, stricken at the thought. He looked down once more at the dead man at his feet and remembered the dying Abbot's final injunction: *'Go back'*.

He stayed long enough for one last look at the fortress rising god-like from the quiet ocean; he wanted to imprint upon his memory every detail of this terrible conflict, he knew the opportunity would not present itself again. Even now the portal he had passed through might have closed, as gradually the atoms drew together and repaired the rent in space and time.

The sky screamed and raged against the fortress. Conrad was oblivious to the waves of raw, invisible energy that swarmed around him. He saw the fortress almost covered by the leeching blackness; but moments later they began to fall away in great swirling masses of ash-grey. The sea took them and devoured them, and did not give them up. The sea was the fortress' greatest ally.

A blazing red sun appeared briefly in the sky, swollen and distended, shedding a baleful light upon the battle. A moment later it was gone, and Conrad the boy/man thought he could detect even a few wan stars overhead. But the ravaging darkness soon closed in, and even this vision was lost to him.

He turned and ran. By now his beard had grown so long that it reached his chest. He could not hold back his panic, and when he found that going down the steep slope was ten times more difficult than the ascent had been, he began to wonder if he would ever return alive to the world he had left. Moving downhill was like pushing against a current. . . a current of time. Each step needed just that much extra effort if he was to reach his goal: the place where he had passed out of one world. . . into another.

Behind him the furious battle continued to rage. Overhead darkness was champion and great shafts of light and energy whipped across the sky. His body burned all over, as if he were on fire. Yet as he made his slow progress down the steep slope, a curious thing began to happen: his step grew lighter, his limbs ached less, and when he reached up to explore his face he discovered that his beard had gone and that only a short stubble remained.

But of course!

If he was moving *back* against the current of time which had propelled the Abbot to his death and himself into manhood too soon, then it was logical to assume that the closer he came to his point of entry into this world, the closer he would come to regaining his true self. Armed with this knowledge, he pushed forward relentlessly.

He soon reached the bottom of the slope, and hurried forward, trying to gauge at which point the damaged interface existed. Then he remembered that it stretched out for some distance; taking the steep side of the 'crater' as a reference point, he stepped boldly forward, moving diagonally towards its sloping walls.

One moment the air was screeching and thundering all around him and his flesh was on fire. The next. . .

Daylight broke over him in a great wave; it almost blinded him. *Thank God,* he breathed, and sank to his knees, exhausted. Great blisters covered his hands. His clothes were in rags. But there was no stubble on his face: he had regained his youth. For one brief moment he thought of the gigantic struggle he had left behind: a conflict such as no man had ever before seen and was never likely to again. And all this taking place scarcely inches away, on the other side of the weakened interface that kept these two worlds apart.

He shook his head, and struggled to his feet. His strength seemed to have left him. He took a sight on the monastery, still visible to his near-blinded eyes, and set off in that direction. He had only managed a short distance through the great dunes of mud when he collapsed, his face half-buried in a shallow pool.

Something flopped around close by his head, making awkward, gasping sounds. He opened one eye. A few inches away one of the tiny man-fish creatures was struggling to survive. Its near-human face mocked him. After a while it ceased struggling and flopped over, its head lolling in the mud.

They stared at each other for a long time.

The sleep of silence

Donella was waiting outside the ruined walls of the monastery. From the window of the Abbot's study she had marked Conrad's stumbling progress through the maze of mud dunes and across the slippery open land. Many times he fell, but managed after a while to regain his feet and press on. Her heart went out to him. What had happened? And where was the Abbot?

She hardly recognized the shambling figure that came towards her. It was not the Conrad she remembered; he seemed almost a stranger. His clothes were in rags and hung upon skin covered with scars and blisters. And his face: surely the agony of centuries was stamped upon it. And to think she had once thought of it as being unproven!

"Oh, Conrad." She wept when he came to her. He stared at her with sightless eyes. He opened his mouth as though about to say something, but no words came. Tenderly she put her arms around him and led him back inside the monastery.

There they both found ample time to weep.

• • •

She nursed him for five long days. His face and hands had been badly burned; his clothes were charred and useless. Firstly she undressed him from these rags and helped him into the Abbot's fine bed; then she set about bathing as best she could his blistered flesh.

He gave no sign that he even recognized her; it was as

190

though his eyes remained fixed upon some deep and private vision. All the time she cared for him he never uttered a word; he behaved like a man struck dumb by some terrible tragedy.

After his return, she found little time for tears. Her task was to take care of him until he was well again, and carefully measure out what little they had in the way of food and drink. She found several useful salves in the Abbot's cupboards and applied them gently to his burns, covering them with dressings torn from the bedsheets. This attention seemed to ease his suffering a great deal; his features relaxed a little and gradually the horror that had been stamped upon his face began to fade. But still he did not speak.

In a frantic effort to find more food she scoured the flooded monastery from one end to the other. She was rewarded with a cask of pickled pork, unopened, which had somehow survived the catastrophe. She made a strong broth from some strips of the meat, added dried herbs from the Abbot's collection, and fed it to Conrad slowly, one spoonful at a time.

Donella herself ate very little. There was barely enough food to keep them alive for more than a week, and Conrad needed nourishment to help him find his strength—and his senses. Meanwhile she wasted slowly, praying that help would not be far off.

She took a pail and sifted the brackish pools of water, which she used to dampen cloths which she held against his fevered brow. At night she sat beside him and hummed softly, or sang pretty snatches and lays: anything at all she hoped might soothe his ravaged soul. Sometimes she cradled him in her arms and whispered soothing, loving words, wondering all the time if he would ever come back to her, or if his mind was sealed for ever by what he had seen.

Sometimes he tossed and groaned and muttered unintelligibly in his sleep, and she lay beside him with her arms around him until these paroxysms passed. Then he would fall back into his trance-like state, and she would snatch some sleep before morning came.

As the days passed by his features continued to grow more relaxed. Once he even smiled at her, and he knew that he had recognized her at last. A little something of the boy she remembered had come back to her, but even this was overlaid by the expression of an older man. And so it would remain for the rest of his life.

●　●　●

The main force of the flood had been broken up by the network of dry streams and rivers that lay in its path long before it reached the coastal villages. The worst hit were the villages lying directly in the path of the advancing wave. Northbridge was completely destroyed. Many lives were lost and valuable property destroyed; the accounting for both would be the work of a year or more. But already such work had been begun.

The vast area of destruction left by the flood was the greatest in living memory. But it was not without some boon: land which had lain dry and idle for three long years of drought began to flourish again, despite the relatively high salinity of the water. And in time the survivors pulled themselves together and began to think about sending search parties north to see if anyone had survived the main front of the flood.

●　●　●

The city of Abingdon had been fortunate; only light flooding had occurred within its boundaries. And the College of Science, situated on high and beautifully landscaped grounds, had not felt the weight of the flood at all.

Roger Asquith had been detained from starting his journey back to the monastery because his horse had gone lame. It was this delay of a day and a half that kept him safe in Abingdon and saved his life. And it was he who led the small band of volunteers from the college to seek out the origin of the disaster.

They rode through a deserted, devastated countryside. And when they finally reached the monastery and saw the mountains of mud and silt piled upon the plain, and the lake in the distance, they knew there was worse to come.

Donella hailed them from the tower.

Asquith was astonished. He could not see how anyone could have survived the full onslaught of the flood.

"Oh, please come up!" she cried. "Conrad is alive! *He. . . is. . . alive. . .*"

Seven colleagues rode with the Scientist; an eighth sat on a tumbril and held the reins of two fine horses. Several corpses were piled in the tumbril.

On hearing the girl's cry Asquith galloped into the grounds of the monastery and almost threw himself from the saddle outside the door of the Abbot's lodge.

He raced up the stairs. Outside, his colleagues entered the grounds at a more leisurely pace, marking the tides of filth swept up against the buildings and the human forms embedded in the mud.

Asquith lunged through the open doorway at the top of the stairs. The first thing he saw was the poor, frightened face of the girl, standing by the window.

"By all that's holy," he whispered. "Is it. . . Donella, the knight's daughter?"

She nodded, tears in her eyes.

"Why, child, you are wasted away to a straw! But thank God you are alive."

She pointed to the bed. Asquith swung around and marched quickly to the boy's side. Conrad lay quietly on his back, staring up at the ceiling. He did not seem to recognize his Master.

Donella said hesitantly, standing beside the Scientist, "He has been sorely hurt, my lord. Once he smiled at me, seeming to know me, but he has not spoken—"

193

Asquith moved a hand back and forth in front of the student's face; there was no change in his expression. The Scientist frowned.

"He did well, my lord," the girl went on. You would have been proud of the way he acted. He saved us. He would have saved more if he could, but—"

Asquith turned towards her. "Tell me, child," he said quietly. "What *did* happen here?"

She shrugged; it was a pathetic gesture. "It was The Wall. You remember The Wall? Well, it. . . broke. Shattered. And a great waterfall poured down into the valley. Then a gigantic wave of water came rushing towards us. Conrad brought me safely here, where the Abbot was hiding—"

"The Abbot? Where is he now?"

Donella shook her head. "That I know not. He went off towards the lake. Conrad went after him, to bring him back. You see, the old man was. . . quite out of his mind, I think. And Conrad said we needed him as a witness. But that was days ago. The way you see him now is only a little better than when he returned. Oh, my lord, if only we knew what happened to him out there!"

"You say he has not spoken?"

"Not a word! Not in five long days. Oh, Master Asquith, do you think he will ever speak again?"

"Not unless we get him away from here," the Scientists said grimly. He went over to the open window and leaned out.

"You, below!" he called out. "Clear the tumbril to make way for the living: we have a sick boy up here. Give the dead a decent, common burial: it will be better than most around here will get." Then he turned back to the room. "Donella, we will need some blankets to make a bed for Conrad in the tumbril. . ."

She looked at him wild-eyed. "But where will you be taking us, my lord?"

He smiled gently. "Why, Abingdon. Where else?"

194

"Abingdon." She repeated the name as though it were a benediction.

Asquith called for two men to come up and lend a hand. Meanwhile, he asked the girl to tell him as much as she could about the nature of the catastrophe. Then, while the tumbril was made ready to transport Conrad, Asquith remounted and rode off in the direction of the lake, to see if he could find some sign of the Abbot.

His search proved fruitless. He passed through the maze of mud dunes and marked their grisly adornments, but he found no sign of the old man. Above the great lake the air was still and peaceful: there was no trace of the shimmering haze the girl had mentioned, and which had so fascinated Conrad.

But I will come back, Asquith resolved. *At some later date.* First, he must get those two young ones to Abingdon and see if he could coax Conrad from his profound silence.

Young ones? Why, after what they had been through they hardly seemed so young any more. *For so does nature often thrust us crudely through life, unprepared. . .*

He turned his horse around and rode slowly back to the monastery.

● ● ●

The dead they had gathered during their trek were given a decent burial. When Asquith arrived back the tumbril had already been fitted out with a deep layer of blankets taken from the Abbot's study, and two men were carefully lifting Conrad into place on his new bed. He made no protest— indeed, as one of them even commented, that he hardly seemed to know what they were about.

When he was settled in, Donella climbed into the tumbril and sat beside him, cradling his head in her lap.

Poor ragged urchin, Asquith thought. One could hardly be blamed for wondering again if she were a girl or a boy, so much had the last weeks taken toll of her youth.

195

She looked up as he rode near: "Did you find the old man?" she asked.

He shook his head. "No, lass, I found no sign of him. Perhaps he is at the bottom of yonder lake by now. The best we can do is get you both back to Abingdon as soon as possible."

She looked down at the blank face of the boy. "He could tell you more, my lord, if he would but speak. Only he knows what happened to the Abbot, and why he came back like this."

Asquith said, "I fear we may have to wait some time before Conrad speaks of these things, Donella. He is in a state of such shock such as I have seen in very few men."

"You mean he has been struck dumb?"

Asquith hesitated.

"I know about such things," she went on, looking down at Conrad and stroking his hair. "He explained this and more to me." How long ago that seemed!

The wheels of the tumbril groaned and they moved off.

The girl looked up, catching Asquith's eye. "My lord, he told me he had many good friends at Abingdon. That they would help me. . . take care of me, and teach me to be a lady. Will they? Will there be fine clothes for me to wear, and—"

"Of course there will. And physicians to help Conrad back to health."

Asquith rode forward, joining his colleagues. "Come, my good fellows: let us hasten back to Abingdon. We have seen as much as we need. There will be time enough for us to return and dig through this debris when we have less urgent business to attend to."

They moved off across the mudflats.

• • •

Conrad felt the rough jolting of the tumbril and smiled. He could feel the warm arms of his lady around him and her chin against his forehead. He did not feel a boy any longer, but rather seemed to have become a man; this latter brought about by some strange adventure which he could not explain.

But in time he would remember clearly. . . what had happened. It would take time to tame the wild jumble of words tumbling around in his head, like a flurry of birds that would not sit still. There was so much for him to tell—so much that Master Asquith and his fellow Scientists would want to hear. Of course they would find his tale difficult to believe; it was this, more than anything else, that held his tongue in thrall. Yet there would come a time when truth would loosen it. But not now. Not yet. It was still too soon for him to form the words he would have to speak.

And in fact many long months were to pass before Conrad would be able to relate his terrifying experience.

Yet even as they bounced along he began to feel the mad tumbling of words inside his mind begin to lessen. This gave him a new courage. He smiled; already the first word had come to him. And even the girl could feel this subtle change take place inside him as he leaned against her.

No sentence yet, only a single word that would, in time, open the floodgate of memory on his tongue. One word, the first word that stood out clear among the tattered ruins of his mind.

Donella.